Sarah Harris is a British author writing YA and commercial fiction. Previously published as Sarah Ball, she had three novels published by Piatkus: *Nine Months*, *Marry Me* and *Written in the Stars*. Sarah lives in Cambridge and has two children.

The Definition of Us

Sarah Harris

piatkus

PIATKUS

First published in Great Britain in 2018 by Piatkus

1 3 5 7 9 10 8 6 4 2

A CIP catalogue record for this book
is available from the British Library.

ISBN 978-0-349-41964-0

Typeset in Baskerville by M Rules

Printed and bound in Great Britain by Clays Ltd, Elcograf S.p.A.

Papers used by Piatkus are from well-managed forests
and other responsible sources.

Piatkus
An imprint of
Little, Brown Book Group
Carmelite House
50 Victoria Embankment
London EC4Y 0DZ

An Hachette UK Company
www.hachette.co.uk

www.littlebrown.co.uk

For Ellie and Sam x

Chapter One

Florence was the first to arrive in group room B. She picked the chair closest to the window and stared out across the scorched, municipal lawn to the manor house on the hill. It was only just visible through a thick cluster of trees and it was angled away from her, as though averting its gaze from the collection of wartime buildings that blighted the bottom of the lane. She imagined several generations of fine ladies occupying the stately manor, standing at the mullioned windows and looking down at the featureless, red brick huts with disdain. The Americans had built them apparently, to be used as a hospital during the bombings of the Second World War. 'Dreadful business,' she imagined one of her ladies saying before sipping a pink gin and looking back to the church spires of Norwich.

It was possibly an even more depressing sight now. The buildings were shabby and the glamorous Americans had long gone, leaving the nylon-clad nurses heartbroken and the pavements spotted with chewing gum. The war-wounded had become the shell-shocked and then the mentally ill. Some time after that the NHS had erected a big blue and white sign by the entrance: MANOR LANE DIAGNOSTIC AND THERAPY CENTRE FOR CHILDREN AND ADOLESCENTS. It had to be a large sign with a name like that. Florence liked to rearrange the letters and find other meanings hidden within the words. *Last Chance Saloon* was her personal favourite. That's what it was after all. Tier four: the final level of the child and adolescent mental health services system. If they couldn't help you here then you were most likely beyond help. A casualty of life as poor and unfortunate as those flown here after D-Day in 1944.

The door swung open and Florence turned to see who'd arrived. It was Andrew, his dark eyes darting anxiously around the room in every direction but hers. He ignored the chairs and paced instead, twisting a section of his curly mop of brown hair and groaning. She would have asked him what was wrong but she'd learnt pretty early on that it's best to leave that sort of question to the professionals.

'One thirty,' Andrew muttered to himself. 'One thirty. I see Howard at one thirty on a Tuesday. Just after lunch and before break. It's written on my planner.' He held up an A4 laminated sheet, located the block of time they were now experiencing then looked at the clock on the wall and twisted his hair again.

Florence understood then. They'd all been told to go to

group room B after lunch and no one had explained why. Andrew was obviously next up to see Howard, the visiting psychotherapist, and making him deviate from his timetable was the human equivalent of derailing a very precise and reliable train. One of those Japanese ones most likely – Andrew would know what they were called.

Wilf was next in. His face was glowing red and his short, blond hair was damp with sweat and sticking up at the top like a cockerel's crest. He'd been having a kick-around with the nursing staff at lunchtime. They couldn't persuade anyone else to join in. Wilf was as clumsy as he was temperamental and the memory of what happened to little Dennis Fairchild was still fresh in everyone's minds.

Dennis came in just behind Wilf, his leg still in plaster and a look of concentration on his face as he negotiated the chairs with his crutches.

Jasper side-stepped around him and took the chair next to Florence. She sat up straighter but didn't look at him. The hairs on her arms stood on end like iron filings reacting to a magnet. She rubbed at them irritably, pretending she was cold.

Jasper stashed his bag under the chair, roughed his hair up with one deft hand movement, then sunk down in his seat. 'What's going on?' he whispered, leaning in towards her. His foot was tapping a fast rhythm on the floor as though he'd been walking quickly and wasn't ready to stop yet. Florence had noticed that in the four weeks Jasper had been there he'd hardly sat still. He fizzed with the same kind of nervous energy that impels stand-up comics to pace up and down. He had the same lively banter too, kidding with everyone, even staff, as though he'd known them for years. Florence had been at Manor Lane for three months and still didn't talk to the staff with the familiarity that Jasper did. On the surface he seemed too perky, too confident, to be a patient at Manor Lane. It was only the hint of nervousness in his energy and his sudden dark moods at mealtimes that gave him away.

She shrugged and looked blank, wishing she could enlighten him, but group meetings were always routine and on timetable. This was a first for them both.

Angela, the senior staff nurse, appeared around the door. She did a quick head count then said, 'Has anyone seen Zoe?'

'She's freaking out in the toilets,' Wilf said, stifling a yawn.

Angela angled her head in the direction of the bathroom, paused for a moment then nodded at the distant to-ing and fro-ing of swear words and the placating tones of a nurse. 'Okay, we'll do this without Zoe. I can talk to her later.' She came in the room and shut the door behind her, then picked the chair closest to it. 'Andrew, you want to come and sit down?'

Andrew shook his head and kept pacing back and forth.

'Alright then.' Angela put her clipboard on the floor then sat forward, her elbows on her knees and her hands resting gently together. She looked at everyone carefully, as though figuring out how best to handle the conversation to come. 'I'm afraid I have some unfortunate news,' she said eventually.

Everyone fell silent.

'As you know, Howard Green, your psychotherapist, comes to visit you all on Tuesdays and Fridays.'

'One thirty. He sees me at one thirty.' Andrew glanced at the hands of the clock as they edged nearer to one thirty-five and coughed sharply, pulling on the collar of his T-shirt as if it were trying to strangle him.

'That's right, Andrew, but unfortunately Howard won't be coming in today.'

Florence felt a twinge of disappointment. Her appointment was at three o'clock and it occurred to her for the first time that she'd been looking forward to it. Howard was different from the other members of staff. He asked better questions and never made a note of her answers. His office didn't have a two-way mirror or a table with a box of tissues. It was just a conversation, and it was always interesting.

Jasper was watching Angela carefully, his eyes narrowed and his head angled to one side. 'Will he be back on Friday?'

She pushed her hair back with her glasses and left them perched on top of her head, then she inspected her hands. 'Um. I think that's unlikely. In fact, it's possible he may not be returning, we're not sure yet, but rest assured as soon as we know, we'll let you know.'

Jasper frowned. 'Is he okay?'

Angela shifted in her seat. 'They're personal reasons. Not something I'm able to talk about right now, but I'm sure he's fine and he's very sorry he had to let you down. I know you all like him very much. Some of you may have had him as a therapist before you came here. You've all taken him into your confidence, and we understand you might feel upset that he's not here to talk to right now. I don't think we'll have a replacement for you by Friday, if one's needed, so I've arranged for Richard, from the Youth Advocacy Service, to speak to you all individually instead. In the meantime if there's anything at all you want to talk about you can always come to the nursing and therapy staff or Dr Wendy.'

'No thanks!' Wilf stood up so suddenly that his chair fell backwards.

'Wilf, sit down,' Angela said, calmly.

'No, what's the point? I've seen enough people. I've had it with this place.'

'I'm sorry you feel like that. I can understand why you're disappointed but—'

Wilf rolled his eyes and stalked wordlessly out. Seconds later they heard the familiar sounds of Wilf punching a door, followed by a scuffle and shouts as the nurses bundled him off to the secure room to calm down.

Angela glanced casually at the clock. 'I think we'll just have a long break time,' she said, picking up her clipboard. 'I suggest you take some time out to gather your thoughts, we'll have our usual debrief at four then you'll be free to go home. Andrew, you want to come and spend some time with me or one of the other nurses?'

Andrew shook his head and backed away from her.

'Okay, you're all off timetable till four then. You know where I am if you need me.' She offered a brief smile around the room and left the door open behind her.

A second later Dennis raised himself up on his crutches and hobbled out as well, pivoting in the direction of the TV room.

Florence glanced from Andrew to Jasper. They looked lost in thought, as though they were struggling to compute this new information and needed a reboot. In Andrew's case maybe even a restore-to-factory-settings. She sighed and picked up her rucksack, fishing her book out of it, then went in search of a beanbag.

Half an hour later, Florence was sitting in the day room reading and rereading the same line on the first page of *The Journals of Sylvia Plath*. Thoughts were racing in her head. Conflicting emotions she was trying to make sense of. Mostly she was disappointed. She could understand why Wilf was annoyed. She'd told Howard everything, taken him into her confidence, trusted him. His presence at Manor Lane made her feel safe and understood, the way a nearby parent does when you're small. She was relying on him to get her through the weekend. He knew it was an important anniversary. One whole year this Sunday. He knew she couldn't face thinking about it, that she needed to keep positive and remember how far she'd come. He'd said he was going to lend her a book he thought she might find interesting. Not another self-help book, not fiction, just something he knew she'd like. He'd captured her interest. She'd been relying on that book. She was going to lose herself in it and let the day pass unnoticed. All she wanted to do was get beyond it and move on. Now she was going to have to come up with something herself.

'Hey.' Jasper walked into the day room and slumped down on the sofa.

Florence glanced at him then back at her book, pointlessly turning a page. She could feel his eyes on her.

'Are you pissed off about Howard?'

She gave up with her book and closed it, leaving it in her lap. 'Yeah, kind of.'

He stared at her a little longer then lay back, resting his head on the arm of the sofa. 'I dunno. Something's obviously going on. It's not like him. He's reliable. He wouldn't just leave without good reason.'

She looked at him then. She knew what he meant, but did Jasper really know Howard that well? He sounded too familiar, even for Jasper, considering he could only have had half-a-dozen sessions with him. Then she remembered what Angela said. 'Did you know him before you came here?'

'Yeah. He's my mum's therapist. Has been for years.' He shifted so he could see her better. 'He takes this stuff really seriously. He wouldn't let us down, I don't get it.'

8

It was true. Howard didn't even like being late. It'd happened twice since she'd been there, neither of which were his fault, but he'd been so apologetic about it. Like he needed to make it clear that he didn't take their sessions lightly. He didn't need to, of course. It was obvious from the way he turned his phone off before they got started, and the way he listened, really listened, and recalled the details of what she'd said even weeks later. 'Yeah, I know what you mean.'

She thought about the last time she'd seen Howard, just a few days earlier. He was sitting on the tatty green chair in the corner of his office, his legs crossed and his fingers linked under his chin as he listened to her. He had a universal look of dad about him. A comfy, soft-round-the-middle sort of man with eyes that wrinkled at the edges and terrible taste in clothes. He was wearing brown corduroy trousers and a sweater with elbow patches, even though it was the start of summer, and his greying, wavy hair was a bit too long, as though it'd been fashionable once and he wasn't ready to admit those days were gone.

Howard had started the conversation by asking, 'What makes you happy, Florence?'

It was a question that had made her prickle with irritation. 'Happy' was such an awful word; so empty and insubstantial that it looked, in Florence's mind, like an insipid balloon, hanging in the air somewhere out of reach. She told him, loftily, that it wasn't a word she'd want to describe herself as. She'd rather be content, hopeful, fulfilled.

'And are you any of those things?' Howard had asked her.

'Not yet,' she said.

'"Not yet",' he repeated, with a surprised raise of an eyebrow as he emphasised the last word.

They looked at each other for a second and then she smiled begrudgingly, as though she'd been tricked. It was only a word but they both knew she'd just admitted something important.

'He's so easy to talk to,' Jasper continued. 'I can tell him anything and I know he won't judge me.'

'Yeah.'

'And there's stuff I want to talk to him about. Stuff no one else would understand.' He swallowed and looked back up at the ceiling.

Florence felt her stomach flip. He looked upset. She wanted to suggest that he could talk to her, if that would help, but Wilf skulked into the room before she could summon up the courage.

He sat down on the end of the sofa, causing Jasper to sit up quickly and move his feet.

'Honest to God, if I see Howard Green again he's gonna get a piece of my mind,' Wilf said, staring menacingly into the distance and shaking his head.

'C'mon, Wilf,' Jasper said. 'You know he wouldn't disappear unless he had to.'

'Oh, whatever. It's a classic example of no-one-gives-a-shit. You know what Andrew's like. You don't go messing

10

around people like that. For years I've met one do-gooder after another, passed about like a parcel no one wants. Kids who fall out the system. We're a problem. They don't want to understand. They just want to get us back in the system so we can all turn out to be good little taxpayers and stop costing them money. I thought Howard was different but clearly not. He's just like the rest. Paid to ask questions, that's all.'

'I don't think you should be mad at him when you don't even know what's going on,' Florence said. 'He might just be dealing with some crisis and be back on Friday.'

Wilf curled his lip, not ready to give up being annoyed yet. 'It didn't sound like it to me. This whole place is full of bullshit. I'm not talking to anyone else. What's the point?' He scowled and ground his foot into the carpet.

Andrew took a sharp intake of breath and turned around, his expression incredulous. 'For goodness' sake, Wilf, what's the matter with you?'

Florence and Jasper looked up in surprise. Andrew never got involved in these discussions. When it came to emotional territory he was the equivalent of Switzerland.

He held a small blue gadget in the air. 'Your iPod battery's at zero per cent.'

Jasper slumped back against the sofa. 'I thought you were about to say something important then.'

'It *is* important. Lithium ion batteries shouldn't be left at zero per cent. They keep discharging and if they drop below their safe operating area they can lose cell capacity

11

and never recover. I'm charging it now.' He ducked under the desk to find a socket.

'Well, thank God for that,' Wilf said with undisguised sarcasm.

Florence could see the irritation building in Jasper's face as he watched Andrew searching through the wires on the floor to find the right one. 'Andrew, I thought you were upset about Howard?'

Andrew flicked on a switch at the wall then turned back to the room. 'I am. I see Howard at one thirty on Tuesdays and Fridays. I'm not seeing anyone else. I like Howard.'

Wilf snorted. 'So what's gonna happen when you rock up next week and there's some new therapist sitting in Howard's chair?'

'That's not an option.'

'Right. So what're you gonna do about it then?'

'I'm going to find Howard.' Andrew shrugged like it was an obvious answer.

Wilf, Jasper and Florence looked from one to the other, their expressions an equal measure of concern and scepticism.

He blinked quickly. 'I'm not seeing anyone else. If Howard's not coming back to Manor Lane then maybe I can still arrange to see him on Tuesdays and Fridays. He takes private patients too.'

'I'm not sure it works like that,' Wilf said.

'Well, how will we know unless we find out?'

'We?'

'Yes, you're going to help me find him, aren't you? We have a right to know what's going on.'

Jasper sat up then. 'You're right. If they knew something they wouldn't share it with us, would they? But that doesn't mean we should just take it. I want to know he's okay and if he's coming back, because if he's not then I don't want to be here. Howard's the only person I can talk to in this place.' He looked at Florence, as though questioning whether she felt the same.

She nodded. She wished Jasper could talk to her but then she remembered all the things she'd shared with Howard. Things she couldn't imagine telling anyone else. The thought of not being able to talk to him again made her feel lost. Like a story ending mid-sentence. She recalled an article she'd read online about 'closure'. It had actually been talking about relationship break-ups, something she'd never experienced herself, but she recognised the truth in it all the same. When someone disappears out of your life without warning you're left feeling like there's still stuff you want to say and questions you want to ask.

'Yeah, well, I'd like to tell him exactly what I think,' Wilf added.

'Then it's a plan,' Jasper said, his face brightening. 'We're going to find Howard.'

'Technically that's not a plan,' Andrew said, sitting back in his chair and dusting off his knees. 'It's an objective.'

Chapter Two

On Friday, Florence walked into the building with a niggling sense of defeat. Usually she'd have a session with Howard in the afternoon. Their conversations always set her up for the weekend. He'd ask thoughtful, philosophical questions she'd spend days mulling over, and he'd reference books and articles and people she'd want to look up. He kept her mind occupied, and he knew she needed that this weekend more than most. She stared at the nameplate still fixed on his office door and looked for other words hidden within Howard Green.

Wanderer stood out a mile.

'You alright, Florence?' a voice said and she jumped and turned around.

Marika was sitting in reception, half hidden behind several bunches of flowers that were adorning the long shelf in front of her. 'Sorry, you need to sign in, don't you? The book's here somewhere.' She stood up and checked between the flowers on the shelf then started shifting papers on her desk.

Florence looked from the flowers to a row of cards lined up on the window ledge. 'Is it your birthday?'

'Yes, but it's actually a double celebration. I'm also having a baby. Thirteen weeks today. I've just started telling everyone.' She straightened up and proudly stroked her tummy which, if it was harbouring a baby, gave nothing away. Marika had the tiny, delicate figure of a dancer and was usually a bundle of energy, power-walking down corridors with her hair swinging as though every day was a deadline. Today she looked pale and tired, the way people did when they were coming down with a cold.

'Congratulations,' Florence said smiling at her. She wanted to say something else but couldn't think what so she scanned the shelf again and saw that the signing-in book was sitting under a pile of post. She gathered up the assortment of jiffy packets, envelopes and cards, ready to hand them over, and a red envelope caught her eye. The handwriting on it was tall and thin, sloping to the right and with extra little flicks at the ends of the words which made them look like they were unravelling in a strong wind. It was Howard's writing. A quick scrawl with his left hand she'd seen him do many times when he'd written things down for her, like Venn diagrams and names for the axes on a bell-shaped curve he wanted her to place herself on, so much more interesting than asking how she was feeling. Being a film buff he also liked to jot down the names of films he thought she should see. *12 Angry Men* was his last suggestion. She thought it sounded like a guy's film and the word *angry* was spiky and off-putting, like *attack* or *vomit*, but then he'd been right about *The Outsiders*. She'd gone straight to the library to order the book after she'd watched that.

'Florence, are you in there?' Marika said, waving a hand in front of her face. When Florence looked up Marika rolled her eyes with mock impatience. 'You're not with it today. I thought I was supposed to be the preoccupied one?'

'Huh?'

'Mumnesia.'

'What?'

'Baby brain.' She pointed again at her flat yet productive stomach. 'When you're pregnant your brain shrinks, apparently. It makes you forgetful and vacant. You don't have that excuse, I'm afraid.' She held out her hand for the post.

Florence glanced at it again, unwilling to let it go. It might contain an address, contact details, even a reason why he'd gone.

Marika gave up waiting for Florence to pass it over and took it out of her hand, then she spotted the signing-in book. 'Ahh, that's where it got to. Give us your signature then.' She held out a pen and gave her a teasing smile. 'If your name's not down, you're not coming in.'

Florence continued to stare despondently at the red envelope, now out of reach on the desk.

Marika tutted. 'Never mind, I'll do it. You'd better get yourself off to the morning meeting.'

Florence was the last person to arrive in the group room.

Vanessa, one of the staff nurses, was taking the meeting and was already seated and smiling expectantly around the room when Florence walked in.

She went to the only empty chair and sat down quickly.

The room was quiet and there was an air of despondence. Jasper, Andrew and Wilf looked in no mood to co-operate. After two days spent trying to gain information about Howard they'd drawn a blank and had to give up. The staff looked cagey and concerned whenever his name came up but they gave nothing away. Not even Aggie, the cook, knew anything and she was usually the eyes and ears of Manor Lane. When staff talked in the kitchen it was like they forgot she was there. She'd often overhear conversations then repeat them later with a conspiratorial, 'You didn't hear this from me but . . .'

When Florence and Jasper had gone to see her on Wednesday morning she'd looked as baffled as they were.

'All I know is that when I got in this morning I found this . . .' She took the lid off the kitchen bin and pointed inside. Sitting amongst a pile of vegetable peelings and an old newspaper was Howard's mug – the one with his name printed on the front. It wasn't even broken. Aggie shook her head and regarded it as if it were the sad remains of an old

17

friend. 'I think it might have been Zoe,' she said. 'She's taken it very personally, bless her.'

Vanessa went over the day's timetable then asked what everyone was up to over the weekend. It was standard morning meeting stuff. They were encouraged to share snippets of their lives with the rest of the group. How their weekend had gone, what they'd done the night before, that sort of thing. It might have seemed like an ordinary conversation if it wasn't for the fact that the nurses took notes. None of them ever gave much away, but with the staff keeping them in the dark about Howard they were even less keen to participate.

'Let's start with you, Florence. Anything interesting planned?'

Florence slouched in her chair and developed a sudden fascination with the multi-coloured fibres in the short, scratchy carpet. 'Not really.'

'Something with your family, maybe?'

She could feel Vanessa's eyes on her, as though she could look right inside her head and see the pictures of her home and family that had involuntarily appeared. There wasn't much to see. It was mainly the view of her bedroom, as seen from her bed in the far corner of the room. At weekends she'd got into a routine of sleeping till lunchtime then getting up to make toast, taking it back to bed and reading until she could tell by the sounds and smells coming from the kitchen that her mum was making dinner. She might have a shower and get dressed then, more to keep her parents from looking at her pyjamas with woeful defeat than because she actually wanted to. She'd have an awkward conversation with them over dinner then go back to her room and watch TV on her laptop till the early hours of the morning. The only noteworthy moments during the previous weekend were that her cat, Watson, caught a frog and left it on the lawn, causing her dad to accidentally mow it, and later on that day she'd looked out of her bedroom window and seen her mum hanging out the washing and trying to hide the fact that she was crying. Florence suspected the two incidents weren't related but couldn't be entirely sure.

'No, nothing,' she said with a shrug.

Vanessa looked hopefully at Andrew instead.

Out of all of them, Andrew was the most likely to talk, being generally under the impression that whatever made his life interesting would be just as interesting for everyone else. Unfortunately, because Andrew didn't have a very interesting life, it meant they were often subjected to stories about articles he'd read in the *New Scientist* or some new discovery that had been on the news. A few weeks ago, he talked for what felt like several hours about the live streaming of a talk Peter Higgs gave at a science festival on the standard model of particle physics. Florence had absolutely no idea what he was talking about most of the time but did manage to figure out two things:

1. Scientists are very interested in stuff that is either too tiny to see or too massive to comprehend.
2. They have some really great words for stuff like *nanobots* and *paradigm*.

Florence had a list of favourite words written in the back of her notebook, words that were pleasing to say, like *shenanigans*, *nefarious* and *snark*. She often made a mental note of the words Andrew used so she could add them to her notebook later. In fact the more time she spent with him, the more her list resembled a glossary in a science book.

Andrew was inspecting his fingernails and Vanessa had moved on to Wilf.

Wilf's contributions varied depending on his mood. Usually he'd be sullen and monosyllabic, but when he was in a good mood he'd chip in with stories about guys doing stereotypically guy things: fishing, football, drinking, fixing up cars, barbecuing steaks ... Florence had this vision of Wilf's life outside Manor Lane being one big bloke fest. Like a stag party meets channel Dave.

He wasn't playing ball today. He sat with his arms folded and looked from Florence to Andrew to Jasper as though making it clear that his silence was an act of solidarity.

Zoe, who'd been watching them too, suddenly stood up and backed towards the door, her eyes wide and panicked.

'What's the matter, Zoe?' Vanessa said, sitting up and looking grateful that something was finally happening.

'They're plotting against me,' Zoe said, pointing a finger at them. 'They want to hurt me. They've been talking all week. They've got a plan.'

'Zoe, no one's got a plan. Why don't you sit back down and tell us what you did last night.'

'No, I don't want to. I don't want to be here.' She turned and fled the room, the door swinging open behind her.

Vanessa got up and pressed the alarm button on the wall then stepped outside.

Florence concentrated hard on the carpet while the sound of the bell droned on, accompanied by footsteps and a mixture of hysterical wailing and calm, mollifying voices. Zoe's paranoid episodes were a regular occurrence but the thought that she might have contributed to one made Florence feel uncomfortable. She didn't want to be responsible for making anyone feel bad.

'Right, where were we?' Vanessa said, walking back into the room and sitting down with the breezy composure of someone who'd just got up to let a cat outside.

Florence could feel Jasper looking at her, trying to catch her eye. She stared out of the window instead, watching a jogger run through the fields in the distance. A normal person doing a normal thing.

She tried to imagine what that must feel like.

Florence's notebook

Awesome words

porridge	snuggle	positron
shenanigans	snark	neutrino
jambalaya	matrix	equinox
malady	moron	zenith
nefarious	nanobot	supernova
hootenanny	quark	

Awful words

soap	sticky	wormhole
poise	vomit	Milky Way
happy	turnip	plasma
perfume	slurp	gluon
cheese	chunks	nebular
discreet	panties	

Chapter Three

When the meeting was over, Florence gestured for Andrew, Jasper and Wilf to wait behind. When Dennis had left the room she told them about the envelope she'd seen with Howard's writing on it.

'So we take it then,' Wilf said, popping some gum in his mouth. 'It'll just be sitting on her desk.'

'I'm not taking her post.' Florence's voice came out too high and too loud. She closed her mouth and looked guiltily towards the door.

Wilf rolled his eyes. 'You're such a goody goody. It's not like it's theft or anything. I'm just talking about reading it. It might give us an idea what's going on.'

It sounded like theft to Florence. The words in that envelope were intended for someone else. Private words. 'But, Marika's always at her desk,' she said.

'She's not,' Andrew said. 'She spends most of her time marching around the building and leaving the doorbell ringing.' His expression suggested this was a major source of irritation. 'We just need to wait till she's running an errand or making a cup of tea or something. I'm sure we won't have to wait long.'

The three of them looked at her expectantly.

'I'll think about it.'

Andrew was right. When they got to the classroom, Tina, the teacher, was standing at her desk, sorting out papers for an English controlled assessment they were doing that morning. They were just taking their seats and emptying their bags when Marika tapped on the door then stepped into the room.

'The photocopies you asked for,' she said, holding out a handful of papers.

'Oh, thanks.' Tina took them then looked more closely at Marika. 'Are you okay? You look a bit peaky.'

'Not really. Aggie's frying onions and the smell just . . . Ugh.' She put a hand to her mouth and exhaled steadily then said, 'Sorry, it's no good . . . ' and rushed out the room, turning right towards the bathroom.

Jasper nudged Florence, looking at her significantly, then Wilf gave an exaggerated cough. Florence didn't need to turn around to know that Andrew was also willing her on.

'Alright, alright,' she whispered under her breath then put her hand up, thinking fast.

'Yes?' Tina said.

'Sorry, I think I might have left my book in the meeting room. Could I . . . ?'

'Sure. Make it quick.'

She left the room, checked the corridor was empty then hurried towards reception.

The door to the office had been left unlocked so she snuck in quickly. The desk was covered in clutter and there were cards everywhere: dotted around the mess on her desk, balanced precariously on the photocopier and lined up high on a window ledge. For such an efficient person, Marika had a surprisingly disorganised workspace. Florence reached for them one at a time, scanning the signatures. She felt wrong, like a peeping Tom, and so she tried to concentrate on the handwriting itself rather than what the words said. None of the cards were from Howard. She scanned the desk, moving papers and lifting a sealed box of chocolates. Howard's red envelope was sitting underneath, the fold on the top ragged from being torn open. She picked it up and turned it over in her hand. It was stiff, as though there was a card inside rather than a letter. She wanted to take it out but couldn't. It was too personal.

She imagined Andrew back in the classroom, his hopes pinned on finding Howard, then she remembered Jasper's face, challenging her. She didn't want to return without news. She stared at the address on the front, as if it could contain some clue, then she spotted a postmark and her heart gave a jolt. There was a smudged, inky ring surrounding the stamp. The post date was clearest. It had been sent the day before. The place name was blurred and illegible apart from the letters *nia*. As she looked at it, trying to figure out the missing letters, the phone burst into life making her jump. She quickly put the envelope back on the desk then heard the bathroom shut at the end of the corridor and Marika's footsteps swiftly approaching. She hurried out of the office and, not wanting to have to explain to Marika why she'd been there, she dived into Howard's office and hid behind the door.

She stood still, her heart pounding as Marika ran to reception to catch the phone before it stopped ringing. She exhaled slowly, realising she was trapped. If she walked out now Marika would see her but if she stayed much longer Tina would start wondering where she was. 'Idiot,' she muttered under her breath.

'Oh, hi, Wendy,' she heard Marika say. 'Aren't you supposed to be in this morning?'

Wendy was Manor Lane's resident doctor. A friendly, caring woman with a desk cluttered with framed photos of children dressed mainly in skiwear. She came across as overworked and short on time. She was often riffling through piles of paperwork as though she'd lost something and would answer her phone in the middle of a consultation then hang up, look bewildered and say, 'Where was I?' Florence's mum thought she was scatter-brained and should be giving them her full attention but Florence didn't mind. It made her seem less intimidating when she talked about medication and therapy.

'Oh I know. It's awful, isn't it? The moment it rains that road's like a car park. Yes, don't worry. I spoke to all the parents yesterday apart from Jasper's mum. I can't seem to get hold of her. I'll keep trying. But yes, they were okay about it. Florence's mum was the most concerned. She was saying how much Florence likes Howard and that she'd really turned a corner with him. She was worried the disappointment might send her on a downward spiral. This is going to be a difficult time of year for her, as you know. Apparently on Sunday it'll be a year since . . . '

Florence took a sharp intake of breath and put her hands over her ears. She looked away from the door and concentrated on Howard's office instead, trying her hardest to block the words out, then Marika said, 'No, nothing new. I got a birthday card from him this morning but it didn't say anything, just a signature. I'm surprised he managed that to tell you the truth; he went so quickly I figured it must be serious. Whatever it is he's not saying, not to me anyway, just that it's personal circumstances and he's staying with his sister for a while. No, the writer. I know they're close – she's the only family he ever really talks about. I know. He's very concerned about the patients. He'd never have wanted to leave like that without even saying goodbye. I just hope he's okay. He spends so much time helping other people, I hope he's got someone looking out for him. Yeah, he is . . . Me? Oh, I'm alright. I've just got the most awful sickness this morning and my head's pounding. Oh right, are they okay to take when you're pregnant then? Are there some in the medical cupboard? Okay, I'll go and get some now. Yes, and I'll hopefully see you in an hour or so. Okay, see you later.' She hung up the phone and there was a rattle of keys then Marika's footsteps retreated back down the corridor.

Florence stood still for a moment, thinking through what she'd heard. Howard was unlikely to be coming back. He was obviously dealing with something difficult. Was he ill? It sounded like he didn't have much in the way of family or anyone to help. She'd never really thought of Howard needing anyone. Her stomach twisted up at the thought of Howard being vulnerable to anything. He was the one who made people feel better. He had to be okay.

She looked around the dark office with a growing sense of unease. There was still a jacket hanging on the back of his chair. He'd clearly left in a hurry. She walked slowly over to his desk. His computer screen was in sleep mode and his answerphone light was blinking. Her eyes cast over the assortment of files on his desk. There were no photos in frames like in Doctor Wendy's office. How had she not noticed that before?

As Florence went over Marika's conversation with Wendy again she suddenly remembered the words, 'on Sunday it'll be a year since . . . '

She tried to shake them out, determined not to think about it, but they lingered with an increasing sense of foreboding.

She spun around and headed back to the door,

closing it quickly behind her before hurrying down the corridor. Perhaps, if she was fast enough, she could leave the words behind.

At break time Andrew practically frogmarched her to the day room, Jasper and Wilf following. Andrew closed the door behind them then they all looked at her expectantly.

Florence didn't know where to start.

'Well?' Andrew said.

Jasper nudged her. 'Come on, Florence, you've been looking worried ever since you got back from the office.'

She inhaled slowly. 'Okay, so I didn't read the card, the postmark had an n-i-a in it if that's any use. Could be anywhere. Then the phone rang and Marika came back so I hid in Howard's office.' She told them about the overheard conversation. 'I'm worried about him,' she concluded. 'He's obviously got something going on, and it doesn't sound like he's got much in the way of family for support. What if he's ill, or depressed or something?'

'Poor Howard,' Jasper said.

'Hmm.' Wilf screwed up his face. 'I dunno. Howard's not the sort to be depressed or anything like that. He's sorted. He's got an answer for everything. He'd just psych himself back on the straight and narrow.'

'I'm not so sure,' Jasper said. 'He told me once that he had depression and anxiety before he went to university. That's why he wanted to be a therapist.'

'He told me the same,' Florence said. 'I always thought it was hard to imagine but no one's immune to it. You can't go by how people come across on the outside.' She thought about what Marika said. 'He was always dealing with other people's problems. That's got to be a hard job for anyone to do all the time.'

'Yeah.' Jasper frowned. 'I feel bad now. He's helped us so much and I've never actually thanked him for it. I should have done.'

Florence felt a pang of guilt. She'd only ever thought of Howard in the context of a therapist. Had she ever asked him how he was doing? How his day had been? 'You're right. We should at least let him know he's appreciated.'

'Here you go,' Andrew said.

They all turned to look at him. He was sitting at the computer desk pointing at the screen. On it was a home page for an art therapist called Angie Hamilton.

Florence peered closer. 'What's this?'

'This is Howard's sister, apparently. You said she's a writer so I Googled her.'

Nothing about the page was familiar to Florence. 'I don't know, Andrew. Howard told me about her once. I got the impression she was a fiction writer.'

'It's definitely her.' Andrew clicked on a link. 'It's written in her blog, see?'

The post was titled 'Book Launch July 26th' and explained that she and her brother 'Howard Green *DClinPsych*' had

30

co-written a book called *Talk and Draw Therapy: Unlocking the Mind* to be published the following month. Beneath the post was a photo of Howard and Angie, dressed up and standing together with drinks in hand, as though at some kind of party or reception.

Andrew clicked the contacts page. 'She works from home. Here's her address. She lives in Cambridge.' He sat back and folded his arms, satisfied.

'Well, that's good,' Jasper said. 'Maybe we should go and see if we can talk to him? See if he's okay?'

'Of course we should,' Andrew said.

Florence laughed nervously. 'Really? Isn't that a bit weird? I was thinking more like posting him a card or a letter or something.'

Jasper shook his head. 'I don't think a card's enough. If we just post something to him and he doesn't reply how will we know he's okay? I think we should find him. What's the worst that can happen, he doesn't want to see us? At least we'll know we've made an effort.'

Andrew was nodding. 'Yes, and then we can get him to come back.'

'Well, maybe not, Andrew. But we could at least let him know he's appreciated, maybe say goodbye.' Jasper looked from Florence to Wilf. 'We should all go. This weekend. What do you think?'

Florence felt a pang of unease. Was it the right thing to do? She thought about the weekend and weighed up the pros and cons. She needed to keep busy. Finding Howard and letting him know how much they appreciated him, that was a positive thing to do. She couldn't have got through the past year without his help. It couldn't just end like this. And doing something positive had to be better than sitting at home feeling sorry for herself. But then what about the others? Did she really want to be hanging out with them outside Manor Lane? What if Andrew had a meltdown, or Wilf chucked a wobbly? She counted up their various disorders. Wilf's ADHD and aggressive tendencies, Andrew's ASD and possible obsessive compulsive disorder, Jasper's eating disorder and her own depression meant they had a total of at least five mental health disorders between four of them. It could be a disaster, and that was before she'd factored in the way she felt around Jasper.

'I don't know, guys. I mean, how would we even get there? I've got no money for a train fare and none of us can drive.' She was half hoping that pointing out the obstacles in their way would take the decision out of her hands.

'I can drive,' Wilf said.

Andrew looked sceptical. 'How can you drive? You've only just turned seventeen.'

'My dad owns a garage, remember? He's been teaching me on the side so I can help out with the business. I took my test just after my birthday and I'm insured on my brother's van.'

'Would he let you borrow it for the day?'

'Probably. He spends most of his weekends down the pub and I'm always giving him a lift back. He owes me a favour.'

Andrew frowned and bit his nails. 'I don't know, Wilf. The statistics aren't good for drivers your age. Do you know how likely you are to die in a car accident?'

'A lot less likely than most, mate. I'm a good driver. Passed first time and I've got no points. I'm not stupid. If anything happened to Mitch's van he'd kill me. Twice.'

'Interesting.' Andrew mulled it over for a moment then said decisively, 'I think we should do it. What do you think?'

Wilf shrugged. 'Look, I don't know about Howard, his life is his business, and I can't see how us turning up will make any difference to anything, but if you need a ride I'll come along. I wouldn't mind getting away from here for the day. The weekends do my head in.'

Florence was surprised by the amount of feeling Wilf put into that last sentence. She'd got the impression it was Manor Lane that did his head in and his weekends were comparatively perfect.

'So are you going to join us, Florence?' Jasper said.

She'd been avoiding catching his eye so far, certain what would happen, and when she eventually glanced his way she was proved right. He was looking at her with the pleading eyes of a puppy.

'Resistance is futile,' Andrew said, with uncharacteristic perception.

'Alright, I'm in,' she said, already worried she was going to regret it.

Chapter Four

It was rare for Florence to be up and dressed before 8 a.m. on a Saturday. As times of the week go, it didn't seem too bad. The work day hum of cars ticking over and the squeals of children walking to school had been replaced by the softer, less urgent sounds of birdsong and the clatter of a letterbox as the postman continued up the street. It was going to be a hot day. Florence could already feel sweat forming on her forehead and the bridge of her nose. She didn't like hot weather. Bright sunshine was too exposing. She liked wearing her hair down and pulling her sleeves over her hands. She liked the weighty presence of Doc Martens on her feet and feeling justified about staying indoors. She'd opted for a pair of low Converse this morning, and the same style skinny jeans she always wore, her biggest concession to the weather being that she was wearing her favourite green T-shirt without her usual hoody or oversized cardigan. To make her feel less underdressed she was also wearing a collection of bracelets, a random mix of coloured beads, hairbands and charity wristbands, including her favourite: a Japanese lucky cat charm on red braided cord that her friend Kimi gave her the day before she went to Manor Lane. She twisted it absent-mindedly around her wrist as she waited.

The sudden roar of a diesel engine broke the silence and a flock of birds took flight from a nearby tree. Florence looked up and saw a van rounding the corner. 'You have got to be kidding me,' she said under her breath as it pulled to a stop beside her.

Wilf jumped out to join her on the pavement. 'What do you think?' he said, patting the side of the van as if it were a prized bull.

'It's, er ...' She cast her eyes over the graffiti art that covered the van. There was a giant, unreadable tag on the side, a sketchy union jack on the bonnet and a gurning bulldog wearing a pair of headphones on the double doors at the back. 'It's very, er ...' There were no words. She held her hands out to depict something that was exploding with visual loudness.

'My cousin did it. He's a legend.'

She took a closer look at the letters in the tag. 'Did he also do the bus stop at Cotman Fields?'

Wilf looked at her, unable to figure out whether she was joking or not, then said, 'Yeah, well, if that doesn't impress you, take a look inside.' He slid the side door open then gestured for her to climb in.

The interior was better than Florence had expected. It was kitted out like a camper van with a C-shaped sofa facing a table at one end and a cupboard and a chair at the other. The panels were painted pale blue and there were union jack curtains hanging at the side windows. It had a hint of a guy's bedroom about it and was full of clutter – mainly fishing, cooking and camping equipment – but the panelling was intact and the seats were clean. 'It's alright,' she said, nodding her approval.

'It gets better,' Wilf said. 'The table folds up, the sofa and chair turn into beds and look . . . ' He lifted up the cupboard top to reveal a small camping stove and sink underneath.

'Wow.'

'This is my baby.'

'You can cook?'

'Yeah, it's kind of my thing.' He said this with a shyness unusual for Wilf, taking Florence by surprise. She'd thought cars and football were more his thing. If she'd given it any thought at all she would have expected him to be most proud of the fold-out beds. The fact that he'd not yet pronounced it a 'passion wagon' was making her question everything she'd assumed about him.

He dropped the lid back down. 'Plus it goes down a bomb with the ladies. Chicks love a guy who can cook, right?'

She rolled her eyes as normality was restored. 'Not if you call them chicks, Wilf.'

*

She sat on a corner of the sofa, which was fitted across the back of the cabin where Wilf was driving, meaning she could see and talk to him without having to sit in the passenger seat and have her face planted on top of a union jack for all her neighbours to see. She almost wished they weren't collecting anyone else. It was comfortable in the back and with Wilf busy navigating she could put her feet up, read her book and pretend she was back in her bedroom.

'Get a load of those houses,' Wilf said with a whistle as they drove through the south side of Norwich. They were heading to Andrew's house next, an address located in the golden triangle of the city, or, as Wilf called it, 'the money plots'.

Florence looked out the side window. 'Is this Andrew's road?'

'Yeah, he's number nineteen.'

She watched as they passed a variety of detached houses, hidden down long drives and masked by the leafy canopies of mature trees, and counted the houses till she got to number nineteen.

'This is the one, look.' She pointed to a red brick house with bay-fronted windows and a large extension over the garage. Two tall bay trees had been placed either side of the porch. They were neatly pruned into the shape of lollipops and reminded Florence of a pair of sentries she'd seen standing outside a guard's hut at Buckingham Palace. The wide driveway had two separate entrances with a perfect semi-circle of green lawn between them. Wilf slowed down and indicated that he was going to pull in.

'Wait. You're not going in there, are you?'

'Why not?'

'Well, they'll see the van ...'

'And? They know we're coming.'

'But ...'

Wilf glanced over his shoulder at her. 'What? You got a problem with the van?'

Florence imagined what her own parents would say if he turned up on their drive in it. Graffiti was up there with tattoos, piercings and Channel 5 documentaries on the endless list of things they disapproved of. 'Come on, Wilf, it looks like a rapper's roadie van.'

'They won't mind. From what Andrew said they're just glad he's got some friends.' He pulled into the first entrance, stopping just in front of the porch, then got out and opened the side door for Florence.

Andrew and his parents must have been looking out for the van because when Florence stepped out onto the gravel drive they were already standing by the porch. Andrew had a rucksack slung over one shoulder and was holding his laptop case close to his chest. He coughed several times, tugging at the collar of his T-shirt, and stared at the van as though he might have had a change of heart.

Andrew's dad stepped forward to shake her hand. Florence had seen him from a distance when he'd been in to Manor Lane for a meeting with staff but she'd never seen him up close before. She was surprised how much he looked like Andrew: tall and pale skinned with the same dark brown eyes and unruly hair, only his was cut a little shorter and had long since turned grey. He had the same awkward formality too but he was friendlier than Andrew, making eye contact as he enthused about Cambridge, talking about his time spent there at university. He started suggesting places to visit, clearly assuming they were going to spend the day sightseeing.

'Well, I guess we'd better get going,' Andrew said, interrupting his dad with the impatience of someone who'd heard it all before.

A long-haired white cat rubbed affectionately against Andrew's leg and he bent and stroked the top of its head fondly, telling it to be good while he was away, then he climbed into the van with only a cursory 'bye' to his parents.

His mum stayed in the drive, watching as they pulled away. She raised a hand to wave them off then wrapped her cardigan tightly around her.

Andrew didn't join Florence at the side window to wave at her. Instead he picked out the chair at the back of the van, placed his things around it, then settled down with his laptop on his knees.

Jasper lived a short drive away in Templemere, on an estate of mainly terraced houses and flats. When Wilf arrived at the address it wasn't clear which of the flats was his. Florence could see number 31 towards the end of a row of terraced houses but not 31B.

Wilf scanned the buildings then impatiently beeped the horn.

'Wilf! It's only half eight. Some people might still be in bed.' Florence cringed as she imagined half the street now standing at their bedroom windows, staring daggers at the graffitied van. 'Does his mum even know we're coming? Perhaps we should text him and say we're outside.'

'Nah. His mum's not even there, apparently.'

'I'll go and knock then,' she said.

She stepped out of the side door and slid it shut behind her, taking in the surrounding streets. The only people she could see were a couple of young children playing with plastic trucks on a nearby driveway. They looked up every now and again, curious about the brightly painted van. The row of terraced houses they'd parked in front of was broken up into flats. The first floor was set back from the ground floor and a low wall hid their front doors from view. 31B had to be one of those. She crossed a patch of grass to a brick stairwell at the end of the building, took the steps two at a time, then turned a corner so she could see the front of the flats and the door numbers.

The muffled sounds of a television was coming from a flat further down; animated men's voices and audience laughter grew louder as she passed the doors, counting until she reached 31B near the end. The flat to its left was boarded up and the flat to the right was the one with the television. It was so loud standing next to it that she wondered why no one was complaining. She raised her hand, about to knock on Jasper's door, then realised it was already open and froze. Her heart sped up. Something wasn't right. It was dark inside, the curtains still drawn, and it was eerily quiet. Then she saw that the doorframe was splintered, fresh shards of wood sticking out at angles where someone had forced against it to open the door.

'Jasper?' she said, her voice timid. 'Are you in there?'

She thought she heard a reply, a voice as quiet and apprehensive as her own. She pushed open the door and peered inside. When she saw Jasper she gasped and turned around, rushing back to the wall. She leaned over it and shouted down to the van. 'Wilf! Get up here quick. I need you!'

Chapter Five

Jasper was sitting in the hallway, leaning against a wall with his legs out in front of him. He might have looked like he'd picked an odd place to sit and wait if it wasn't for the cut on his cheek and a deep red bruise forming around it.

Florence bent down in front of him, her stomach taking a dive when she saw him up close. 'What happened? Are you okay?'

'Sorry, is it time to go already?' He rubbed his face, as though he'd just woken up, then sat forward and looked at his watch. As he did so he winced and tentatively touched the back of his head.

'Jasper, do you need an ambulance?' Her hands were trembling as she took out her phone. 'I think I should call someone. What about the police? Have you been burgled?'

He shook his head then closed his eyes and sat very still for a moment, as though he'd made himself dizzy. 'No, don't call anyone. I'm fine. Just . . . Can you give me a minute?' He held out his hand and she slowly helped him up.

Wilf and Andrew came rushing in through the door then stopped just as quickly.

'Oh no,' Andrew said, looking from the splintered door frame to Jasper. 'Oh dear.'

'It's okay, honestly. I'm alright,' Jasper said, holding his hands up. 'Don't panic. I'm ready to go, I just need my bag. It's in the kitchen.' He staggered towards the kitchen door and Florence took his arm, steadying him. She glimpsed through a door leading into the living room and saw that a table had been turned over. Its contents had spilled across the carpet, including a mug of tea. They walked into the kitchen but there were no signs of a struggle in there. She pulled a chair out from under a table and sat Jasper down on it.

Wilf followed them, his phone also in his hand, ready to call for help. 'Mate, what's going on?'

'Please, don't call anyone. It's fine, seriously.'

Andrew stood in the doorway looking at the mess in the living room. 'Oh dear,' he said again, wringing his hands.

'Of course it's not fine,' Florence said. 'Someone's broken in and you look like you've been beaten up. We need to get help.' She couldn't believe he was being so dismissive. The thought of him being hurt churned her up so much she wanted to cry and rage all at the same time. She wanted to know that whoever did this was going to be caught and locked up and never go anywhere near Jasper again.

'Look, you can't tell anyone.' He put his head in his hands and exhaled before looking back at them seriously. 'It's my mum. She owes these guys money. They came this morning and took some things. They found a box on the mantelpiece with her wedding ring and some other bits of jewellery, things from my gran that mean a lot to her. I tried to stop them. They got a bit heavy with me, that's all.'

'They can't do that! There's laws against that stuff,' Florence said. 'They need a warrant or something, don't they? They can't just get violent with you.'

'They're not exactly the sort of guys who stick to the rule book. You can't call the police. It'll just make things worse, trust me.'

'But, what about your mum? Where is she?' Florence remembered the conversation she'd overheard at Manor Lane, when Marika said she'd been unable to get hold of her.

'She's in Spain. Has been for a while. She's got a job out there.'

'So she just left you with her mess to deal with?'

'I guess so.'

'Jeez.' Wilf looked like he was ready to punch a door again.

'Hey, it's not all bad. She left me twenty quid for food. That'll keep me going for months.' Jasper's laugh didn't quite reach his eyes.

Florence sat down in front of him. 'Look, what should we do? We want to help you, but I don't know what's best. Do you want me to call my parents, or Wilf or Andrew's?' She secretly willed Jasper not to opt to call her parents. They were likely to freak out for a whole variety of reasons.

'No, definitely not. I don't want any more trouble. I just want to get out of here, and I want to see Howard.'

'He's right. Let's not hang around here.' Wilf looked at the front door still swinging open. 'I've got a toolbox in the van. I can fix up the door so it's secure.'

'Thanks,' Jasper said.

'I'll make us a cup of tea or something then, while Wilf gets that sorted.' Florence got up, wanting to do something useful.

Andrew checked his watch and said 'Oh dear' again and Florence realised what he was worrying about then.

'Don't tell me, you've made a schedule and this wasn't on it.'

Andrew scanned the lino floor and looked uncomfortable.

'I think you need to factor some contingency into your plans, Andrew. With the four of us going anywhere, it's pretty inevitable that stuff's gonna happen.'

He was shifting restlessly from one foot to another. 'Hmm. I might go get my laptop out of the van.'

'Yeah, do that.' Anything that stopped him stressing about time had to be a good thing.

Florence found a bag of frozen peas and a tea towel to wrap them in and gave it to Jasper to hold against his cheek, then she opened cupboards and drawers, finding mugs and spoons, tea bags, sugar and half a packet of biscuits. She realised she was moving around the kitchen like she'd been there before. It felt lived in and friendly, with colourful mugs on hooks and chairs and shelves painted pastel colours. Every surface was cluttered with notes and knick-knacks. When she went to get the milk she paused at the door of the fridge. There were pictures of Jasper on it. In the most recent one he was wearing a school uniform, posing for a photographer as though he didn't want to be there. His expression reminded Florence of how he looked during mealtimes at Manor Lane. In another photo he looked maybe a year or two younger, his face less angular, his hair longer and less styled. He was standing centre stage after some kind of drama performance, holding his hands in the air with a cast of others as though ready to take a bow. A third picture was much older. He was a boy, maybe eight or nine, sitting on an attractive older woman's knee, presumably his mum, and he was beaming at the camera, biscuit in hand. Florence stood momentarily mesmerised by these little snippets of Jasper. She wanted to take the awkward school photo away and replace it with one where he was smiling and giving it some swagger. The Jasper she knew best.

Jasper wasn't saying much. He was sitting hunched at the table, frowning into space. The silence was making Florence anxious. He was never this quiet. He was usually the reassuring one. He could make her mood lift just by walking in a room. Yes, he had problems, they all did, but he seemed better at handling them somehow. It was almost like he could switch them on and off.

She fetched the milk and turned back to the counter, realising that she was doing exactly what her mum would do in a crisis. She was keeping busy, making a nice cup of tea, hoping that by not confronting problems they might magically disappear. She placed the mugs between them on the table and sat down opposite him. She wanted to say something to make it better. To coax a smile off him the way he usually could with her, but as usual the right words stayed trapped in a jumble inside her head.

'How are you doing?' was the best she could manage.

He caught her eye and they stared at each other for a moment. She saw a genuine sadness in him and her stomach knotted, but then his expression changed to a look of resignation, and finally the hint of a smile. 'Yeah, I'm alright,' he said. 'I'm just a bit peed off, I suppose.' He lifted his face off the bag of frozen peas and his smile widened.

'Very funny.'

'You reckon I could carry off the hard man look? A sidekick in a gangster movie maybe?' He raised an eyebrow, but even with the bruise he just looked boyish and cute.

Florence felt the knot in her stomach loosen a little. He was doing her job for her. Jollying himself out of his own dark mood. 'I think this is more like a scene from a Marvel comic. Before the industrial accident that gives you a super power.'

'Ahh.' He nodded. 'You mean when the hero's still weedy and pitied by girls?'

'Something like that.'

'Maybe I should start hanging around a few more secret government labs then.'

'Good idea.' She picked up her cup of tea and smiled behind it. 'Maybe just wait till there's a thunderstorm.'

An hour later Wilf had fixed the front door, Jasper had cleaned up the living room and Florence had washed their mugs and made the kitchen look like they'd never been there. They stood at the kitchen door, waiting impatiently as Andrew held up his hand and finished typing on his laptop with the other. 'Two more minutes.'

Wilf's mobile phone buzzed. He took it out, frowned at the screen then quickly put it back in his pocket. 'Now or never, pal.' He turned and headed for the door.

Andrew, who had never been very good at stopping one task and starting another, especially when it involved turning off a computer, looked momentarily torn. When he saw that Wilf was already heading out the front door he sighed and closed it down. 'Alright, alright, I can do it in the van.'

Florence and Jasper sat facing each other on the long seat behind Wilf whilst Andrew was once again settled in the chair at the back of the van, his laptop on his knees.

Now that Florence was sitting down with nothing to keep her busy she realised that she was running on adrenaline. Her heart was beating faster than usual and her hands were trembling. She hoped the vibrations of the van would be enough to disguise it.

Jasper was staring into space. Florence kept stealing glances at him, hoping to catch a glimpse of his usual self. A teasing glint in his eyes. A suggestive raise of an eyebrow. An easy smile. She wanted to reach out to him, break the tension by starting one of their jokey, silly conversations, but she couldn't be sure it'd work this time. She'd never seen him this serious before.

Jasper looked up suddenly, done thinking, and caught her eye.

Florence tried to convey all her thoughts at once in one tentative smile. *I'm sorry this happened. I'm here for you. We'll make it okay.*

He nodded, as though he understood, and as quickly as a switch being flipped he was Jasper again, his eyes bright and playful. He sat forward and tapped out a drum roll on the table. 'Right, it's time for an ultimate question. Which superhero would you be and why?'

Florence laughed with relief.

This was a classic conversation opener at Manor Lane. It was an unwritten rule that when the staff left them to their own devices, and they could talk about whatever they wanted, they avoided discussing the reasons why they were there or anything personal or sensitive. Instead they spent hours in the day room hotly debating their answers to what they called 'the ultimate questions'. They were irreverent and inconsequential and focussed mainly on the kind of classic pop-culture debates that could never be settled with a definitive answer. They broke the ice and gave them something to think about. Something other than their own lives. They covered subjects like: *Favourite Harry Potter spell? Microsoft versus Apple? What order should you watch* Star Wars *in?* And *What the hell is up with sheep anyway?* (A bewildering preoccupation of Wilf's). The only subject that was off limits was *Doctor Who*. In Jasper's first week he'd questioned Andrew's conviction that David Tennant was the best Doctor. The debate had dragged on for two days and culminated in Andrew having to be escorted to the soft room.

'I'd be Batman,' Wilf called out from the front. 'Who wouldn't want to be Batman? A billionaire with a kick-ass car.'

'No, I don't mean who do you *want* to be,' Jasper said. 'I mean, who's most like your personality?'

'Still Batman. I may not have the car yet but bear with me guys, these things take time.'

'I'm not sure, Wilf. Don't you think you might relate more to a character like the Hulk? No offence intended, obviously.' Jasper winked at Florence.

Andrew looked up indignantly. 'He's nothing like Hulk. Bruce Banner is a brilliant physicist who invented a gamma bomb. Wilf's got more in common with Thor.'

Wilf glanced over his shoulder. 'You want me to pull over and give you a slap?'

Andrew gave a small smile as though Wilf had just proved his point then looked back at his laptop.

'Who do you think I'd be?' Jasper said to Florence.

'Spider-Man,' she said, without even having to think about it.

His grin widened, as though she'd just given him a compliment, and she suddenly felt exposed, like she'd told him an embarrassing secret.

Florence hadn't really liked the Spider-Man films until recently. She'd always been slightly irritated by the hyphen. Then, a few months ago, she'd given in and watched the film with Andrew Garfield in it and saw a different kind of appeal. She could forgive the unnecessary, hero-reducing hyphen after that.

When Jasper had arrived at Manor Lane her first thought was that he looked like a skinny Andrew Garfield. He had the same thick hair, styled to look like he'd been buffeted by a cross wind, and his mouth had the same kind of endearing Cupid's bow, slightly angular and pouty. The kind that kept catching your eye and distracting you. Maybe that was why it'd taken several days before she could pluck up the courage to talk to him.

'Spider-Man, the wisecracking boy-next-door,' Andrew muttered, nodding to himself. 'Sounds about right.'

Jasper pretended to frown at Andrew but he still looked pleased. 'What about you, Florence? Who would you be?'

'Oh, I don't know.' She looked away. 'I don't think I want

51

to be a superhero.' She felt like saying it was easier to relate to the one in trouble. The one in the burning building. Instead she said, 'Maybe I'm more of a sidekick.'

'Oh, you mean like Mary Jane?' He tilted his head and waggled his eyebrows at her.

Her cheeks heated up like she actually was in a burning building.

'Robin, maybe,' she countered, in an attempt to look less obvious.

'If you don't like the limelight you could always be Susan Storm,' Andrew said. 'You could turn invisible and save the world without anyone even knowing you were there.'

Florence grimaced at the name. It was soft and ineffective, like the words *blouse* or *murmur*. 'You know who I've always wanted to be?' She smiled then, remembering the old film she'd watched one rainy afternoon when she was still at primary school, young and easily influenced and convinced she was going to be a writer. 'Lois Lane. Superman's girlfriend. Not because of that but because she was so feisty and funny and she had this really interesting job. And I love her name. Howard once told me that she was named after Torchy Blane, a reporter in a bunch of B movies in the thirties. I looked it up and he's right. He's always right, of course. Plus, the character is also based on a real life reporter called Nellie Bly. She pretended to be mad so she could investigate mental institutions. She's so interesting, and they all have these great names. Lois Lane, Torchy Blane, Nellie Bly . . . '

She was animated now, savouring their names as they rolled off her tongue like a chef recounting the ingredients of a signature dish. She realised Jasper was looking at her with an expression of surprise, as though he hadn't realised quite how mad she was until then. 'I suppose I just always liked Lois Lane,' she said, casting her eyes towards the front window, feigning interest in the road ahead. 'More than the superheroes anyway.'

Wilf gave a whistle. 'Shit a brick, you've just out-geeked Andrew.'

Florence bit her lip and vowed to keep her thoughts to herself next time – then Jasper nudged her foot under the table.

'Can I change my mind?' he said, so only she could hear. 'I think I'd like to be Superman.'

Florence's notebook

Top Ten Favourite Character Names

1. Lois Lane
2. Torchy Blane
3. Sherlock Holmes
4. Boo Radley
5. Charlie Bucket
6. Pippi Longstocking
7. Holden Caulfield
8. Rita Skeeter
9. Huckleberry Finn
10. Daenerys Stormborn of the House Targaryen, First of Her Name, the Unburnt, Queen of the Andals and the First Men, Khaleesi of the Great Grass Sea, Breaker of Chains and Mother of Dragons

Chapter Six

They spent the rest of the journey to Cambridge discussing favourites: favourite TV theme tune, favourite dunking biscuit, favourite celebrity voice. They did impressions of their favourite film stars and Florence and Jasper laughed so hard at Andrew's impression of Forrest Gump that Wilf had to pull over so he could see for himself.

Their laughter only dissolved when they stepped out of the van onto the top level of a multi-storey car park, just around the corner from Angie Hamilton's address.

Florence walked over to the railings and leant on them, taking in everything, from the view of the rooftops and spires and the glimpses of green spaces in the distance, to the alleyways behind a row of shops beneath her, where pigeons were nesting over the bin stores, cooing from the holes in the brickwork. The sun was strong but a fresh breeze ruffled her hair.

'Standing in this car park, with the sun on my shoulders,

I feel like a free man,' Jasper said, in the Morgan Freeman voice he'd been attempting to perfect in the van. He was leaning on the wall beside her, looking into the distance and nodding as though he'd suddenly gained an extra thirty years' life experience. Florence almost bought it for a moment – the sad reflection in his eyes, the beaten-but-still-standing body language – then he looked at her and cracked a smile.

'You're going to get an A* in drama,' she said seriously.

'And then I'm going to Hollywood, but first we find Howard.' He turned away from the view and started to cross the car park at a jog, singing the *Les Mis* show tune 'Bring Him Home'.

Florence laughed and Wilf shook his head. 'They seriously need to review his medication.'

They stood outside a three-storey, cream-painted town-house. It was a pretty building with elaborate iron handrails leading up a small flight of steps to a faded blue front door. There were terracotta pots of summer flowers by their feet that smelt of compost and honey. A poster in the front window advertised a bring-and-buy sale that was raising money for a children's hospice. Florence noticed the date and her stomach flipped at the unwelcome reminder. It was for Sunday.

Wilf hung at the back, his thumbs tucked into the front pockets of his shorts. He was frowning; his eyes fixed on a glimpse of the park at the end of the street where people were playing Frisbee and sharing picnics.

Andrew was standing on the top step, his hand hovering over the doorbell and his nose wrinkled as he stared at it with suspicion. It was tarnished and stained from years of use.

Florence stepped up to press the bell for him then returned to the bottom of the steps to join the others.

There was a muffled exchange of voices inside.

'Can you get that? I'm in the middle of something.'

'Angie!'

A child squealed. 'Muuum!'

Eventually soft footsteps approached and a woman opened the door.

She stood looking at them with a frazzled expression. 'Yes?'

Florence recognised her from the website. Her hair was bushier and her face was bare of make-up but she was still recognisably Howard's sister. She looked as though she'd been baking. Her cheeks were flushed pink and there was a spattering of flour on the side of her skirt.

'We're looking for Howard Green,' Andrew said bluntly.

'We're from Manor Lane,' Florence added. 'We heard he was staying with you and wondered if we could see him?'

She looked surprised for a moment, then confused. 'Howard? My brother? What makes you think he's here?'

'Well ...' Florence glanced at the others to join in and help her but they were studiously looking in other directions.

'You see, he hasn't been in this week and we heard a member of staff saying he was staying with his sister. A writer. So we found your address on the internet. I hope you don't mind. We just ... we wanted to see him.'

Angie was looking at them with such a bewildered expression that Florence found herself running out of breath and words.

'I think you might be mixing me up with our sister, Margot. I only dabble. I'm actually a therapist. Margot is the real writer. But ... She lives in Wales.' She paused and frowned, thinking for a moment. 'I don't know anything about Howard going to Wales. Are you sure you've got that right?'

Florence nodded. 'They called a meeting to say he wasn't going to be in. It was kind of out of the blue. I think ...' Florence bit her lip, unsure how much to say. It felt like she was spreading rumours. Gossiping. Maybe Howard hadn't told Angie for a reason? She remembered Marika saying the sister he was staying with was the only member of his family he really spoke about. She wanted to stop speaking but she'd gone too far now. 'The thing is, it sounded like he might not be coming back, like maybe there was a problem, so we wanted to make sure he was okay, and if he's not coming back, say goodbye.'

Angie chewed on the bottom of her lip, thinking this over, then gave a sudden, brisk smile. 'Well, I'm sure he's fine. He's probably just having a break. I'm always saying he gives too much to that job. I'll give him a ring.' She looked as though she was going to head back inside then realised they were still waiting, unsure what to do. 'I'll tell him you asked after him, shall I? I'm sorry you had a wasted journey.' She was still smiling but there was a hint of worry in her eyes. She said goodbye in a rush then went back inside, closing the door behind her.

Florence turned back to the guys. 'Great. Now what?'

'This is weird.' Jasper kept looking at the closed door, puzzled.

Wilf tutted and threw his hands in the air. 'Fuck this. I'm gonna get some food.'

'Hang on.' Andrew followed after him as he started up the narrow street. 'You're not just going to give up now, are you?'

'You heard her. If he's staying with his other sister then that means he's in Wales. You know where Wales is, right? It's the other side of the country. It *is* another country.'

'It's not that far.' Andrew looked at the others as though expecting them to back him up.

Florence shrugged. She wasn't sure exactly how far it was but she doubted they'd get there and back in a day.

'Wilf, please.' Andrew tugged at his arm.

'Andrew, let him get some food then we'll work something out,' Jasper said, jerking his head to indicate that he should hang back with him and Florence and be patient.

Andrew looked as though he was about to argue so Jasper looked at him more seriously and whispered, 'You know what Wilf's like when he's hungry.'

The penny dropped and Andrew slowed down, letting Wilf lead the way. They all remembered Wilf's now legendary rage when they'd gone to Hoveton Hall Gardens for a day trip and the tea rooms had been closed for a refurb.

They sat outside a café in the shadow of a row of ancient college buildings. Wilf was devouring a toasted cheese and ham sandwich and Jasper was nursing a mug of tea and impatiently tapping his fingers against the cup. Andrew had refused any suggestion of food or drink. He was too absorbed with his iPad, trying to find evidence of Howard's other sister.

Florence held her own mug of tea in both hands, keeping it close to her, and looked up at the colleges through the steam. Her unease about Howard was growing. The look on Angie's face had made her more certain that whatever was going on with Howard wasn't good. She was too quick to look worried, as though she knew something they didn't.

Florence glanced at Jasper, worried about him too. His mood was much like the weather they were experiencing. A bright, warm sunshine that made everything glow and sparkle, only to be suddenly eclipsed by a cloud.

Andrew tapped his screen and sat up. 'I think this is her. Margot Green, a Welsh naturalist and writer.'

Wilf recoiled. 'Ugh. Why would you? Especially in Wales. It rains all the bloody time.'

Florence shook her head at him. 'A naturalist, Wilf, not

a naturist. Someone who studies nature. With their clothes on.' A memory came back to her. Howard had said that his sister was a loner who preferred animals and nature to people. They'd been talking about communicating. He was exasperated that she didn't own a phone. That she lived in a fantasy world devoid of people. 'Yes, I remember now. Didn't she write something about dragons?'

'*The Dragons of Bryn*,' Andrew said, turning his iPad briefly to show them a book cover on a page from a bookshop website. 'She's got a site link.' He clicked on it and frowned at the screen before reeling back as though he'd seen something terrible. 'Oh dear me.'

Florence leaned over so she could see what he was looking at. It was a simple website with a detailed dragon illustration for a header and several pictures of book covers next to quotes. 'What's so bad about that?'

'It's awful. Just horrible. It's a frame-based static page for a start. The font needs anti-aliasing, there's no user interface to speak of and it's written in JavaScript.' He shook his head with disdain. 'It's like 1998 all over again.'

Wilf tutted and pointed the crust of his sandwich at him. 'You. Are a massive dork.'

Andrew ignored him and returned to the search engine, clicking on a different link which opened up a newspaper website. 'That's more like it.' He scrolled down a story titled: LOCAL AUTHOR RECORDS FIRST SIGHTING OF RARE BUTTERFLY and pointed mid-sentence, reading aloud.

'Although Ms Margot Green is a renowned naturalist she is perhaps best known for her children's series, *The Dragons of Bryn*. Her popular fantasy stories were said to have been inspired by the picturesque surroundings of Borth y Castell in Snowdonia, where she has lived for over twenty-five years.'

'Snowdonia!' Florence pointed a finger at Andrew. 'It must be right. Remember Howard's postmark ended in n-i-a?'

Andrew pressed his lips together and started typing again, then tapped the screen several times before putting it down on the table. Displayed on the screen was a map of Borth y Castell. It was a small cluster of houses surrounding a narrow coastal inlet. 'There you go. It's a small village and she's well known. All we need to do is go in a local shop or a post office and ask. Someone's bound to know where she lives.'

Wilf chewed his sandwich and regarded Andrew with amusement. 'You actually want to go today?'

'Of course I do. Our objective is to find Howard. We haven't achieved that yet.'

Florence looked at her watch. 'Hang on. Even if we left right now we wouldn't get there till late afternoon at the earliest. We'd either have to drive back in the middle of the night or stay somewhere and I don't know about you but I've not got much money and no, you know, stuff.' She thought about all the things she liked to have with her when she stayed anywhere: toothbrush, deodorant, clean underwear, medication ... 'Wouldn't it be better to go home and think about it? Maybe email her or something?'

Jasper frowned at the mention of going home and turned to Wilf. 'Did I see a tent in the van?'

'Uh huh. Two man, plus the sofa in the van sleeps two and the chair at the back folds out into a bed.'

'So we just need to find a campsite, which wouldn't cost much, and we'd need some money for fuel.'

'I've got money,' Andrew said. 'I can pay for fuel or whatever you need.' He was looking at Wilf with desperation again.

'A road trip. Sounds good to me,' Jasper said, shrugging. 'We've come this far. We may as well keep going.'

Florence looked at him sceptically. 'Isn't that what Thelma said to Louise just before they drove off a cliff?'

He thought about it for a minute. 'You know, this whole thing is kind of reminding me of *The Wizard of Oz*. Howard is the wizard and ... '

'If you say I'm the brainless one I will bash you,' Wilf said, not looking up from his phone.

'It is though, don't you think? The four of us looking for Howard, like we all need him to help us in some way.'

Wilf shook his head. 'Speak for yourself, Dorothy.'

Florence was starting to think she had been transported, Dorothy-like, into a parallel universe; a place with strange, nonsensical characters and an underlying sense of foreboding.

'Come on, Wilf. We can't leave it like this. We have to find him now.' Jasper nudged him and pulled the kind of expression Florence would have found impossible to say no to.

Wilf put his phone away and stood up. 'I suppose I haven't got any better offers on the table. Anybody want to get some supplies before we go? There's a shop just over there. I'll need more food if I'm gonna be driving all day.'

'Oh yes, and I'll need a toothbrush, and some hand wipes if I'm staying in your van.' Andrew picked up his iPad and swung his rucksack onto his shoulder.

'Hang on. Are you sure this is a good idea?' Florence could feel panic setting in. Did she really want to spend the whole weekend with them? Would her parents even let her? She'd told them she was at Kimi's house catching up on schoolwork. If they knew she was considering driving across the country in a van with a bunch of guys from Manor Lane they'd freak for sure.

'Call them now,' Jasper said.

'You want us to get you anything from the shop?' Andrew said.

'Just, wait a minute.' She thought quickly. Tomorrow was the anniversary. A day that had been looming in the back of her mind like an approaching storm cloud. Would she be okay? What if she wasn't?

Jasper nudged her arm. 'Come on, Florence, we need you.'

Her skin prickled. She remembered the concern in Marika's voice and on Angie Hamilton's face. Jasper was right. They couldn't go home now. 'Okay.' She took her purse out of her bag and held it out to him then found her phone. 'Can you get me a toothbrush as well? There's a tenner in there. I just need to call my parents.'

'Alright then.' Wilf clapped his hands together and beckoned the guys to follow him. 'Let's get this freak show on the road.'

'The yellow brick road,' Jasper said, winking at Florence before turning to follow Wilf.

Chapter Seven

Florence called Kimi first. She answered after just two rings and Florence relaxed a little at the familiarity of her voice. She always spoke quickly, with clipped words and bright vowel sounds that made her sentences flicker like a light bulb in Florence's head.

'Florrie, oh my God that's so weird, I was just thinking about you. How're you doing? It's been ages.'

It'd been a fortnight since they'd last spoken on the phone. It didn't feel like ages to Florence, but then time had been playing tricks on her for the past year, rushing ahead when she wasn't ready and slowing to a crawl on the most difficult days.

'Yeah, I'm okay, you know.' She scratched at something on her knee that wasn't really there.

'So, you're feeling better? Are they going to let you out soon?'

She made it sound like Florence had been locked up against her will.

'I've got another four weeks left, then they either sign me off or sign me up for another eight weeks.'

'Oh, you don't want that. You've got to be out for the summer. If they sign you off you'll only miss a few weeks of the holidays. We'll still have loads of time to meet up and do stuff.'

'Fingers crossed.' Florence felt like she had to say that, but the truth was she wasn't sure she was ready to leave Manor Lane yet. The routine was a drag and it was ten times worse without Howard. The group therapy was embarrassing and the family therapy was torture but she'd got used to Jasper, Wilf and Andrew. They were flawed and different and felt more like her than anyone else she'd met. They were the kind of characters she looked for in the books she read and the films she watched late into the night: people she could relate to, not the kind of polished facades you see on Facebook statuses and on the faces of the girls in college when they bunch together at lunchtime and laugh like everyone's watching.

'Speaking of meeting up and stuff, you want to come over tonight? The olds are going away for the night so I'll have the house to myself. Alice is bringing a bunch of scary movies and we're going to order in some pizza and make it an all-nighter. Like old times. Jess is coming too. I'm sure they'd love to see you.'

They both knew she'd say no to that. She wasn't ready to face the others yet. Alice was nice but adding Jess to the mix was like putting Mentos in a bottle of Coke. Florence always felt like she was bringing the mood down when they were together. She tried to feign interest in her constant boy talk and join in with the peals of laughter but she was about as natural as her dad dancing at a wedding. 'Sounds fun but I've kind of got plans this weekend.'

'Oh.' The surprise in Kimi's voice was obvious. Florence never usually had plans of any kind. 'You doing anything nice?'

'Well, I'm not sure about "nice". I'm actually going to Wales with some of the guys from Manor Lane.'

'Oh, you mean like a therapy thing?'

'No, not really. It's just me, Jasper, Andrew and Wilf. Wilf's driving his brother's van and we're camping. We're only staying one night.'

'Right, so you're not going with staff or parents or anything?'

'No.'

'Just you and a bunch of guys in a van? Are you sure?' She made it sound like the precursor to a missing girl story on *Crimewatch*.

'Yeah, but it's okay. They're harmless. Jasper's really nice, Andrew's a science geek and Wilf's alright if you ignore the letchy comments and don't wind him up. He's loads calmer since they upped his meds.'

'Wow. Are you sure you wouldn't rather come to mine? What about your parents, are they cool with it?'

'Actually, that's why I called you.' She chewed on her lip as she waited for the penny to drop.

'You mean you want me to cover for you?'

'Only if they ask. They probably won't, but if I could tell them I'm staying at yours tonight it'd make life way easier.'

'Oh, I dunno, Florence. What if something happens? I mean, are you sure you're okay? It must be tough for you this time of year. Isn't it tomorrow that—?'

Her heart lurched. 'I'm fine. I just need a break. My parents are pretty hard to be around right now and I don't want to keep being reminded. It'll be good to be with people who understand.'

'I understand, you know.' She sounded hurt.

'I know you do.' There was an awkward pause and Florence could feel her hands getting clammy. She didn't want to stay on that subject.

A voice called out 'Kimiko' in the background.

'That's my mum. My parents are leaving now.' She sighed. 'Alright, if anyone asks you're at mine. Just promise you'll look after yourself, won't you? And text me.'

'I will. Thanks.'

'And next week you can fill me in about your new friend Jasper. He sounds interesting.' Her voice was loaded with suggestion.

Kimi had always been able to read her like a book.

Florence pretended she hadn't heard and said goodbye, then she took a deep breath and dialled her parents' number.

The conversation barely lasted more than a minute. Her mum had actually sounded relieved. It'd been over a year since she last stayed at Kimi's house but before then it'd been a regular occurrence. Florence could tell what she was thinking. She was thinking that maybe things were starting to get back to normal at last. Florence felt a twinge of guilt for lying to her.

Once she'd said goodbye she held her phone in her lap and looked across the street to the shop where the guys had gone. She thought she could see them in a queue at the checkout behind the large glass window but then a group of tourists gathered in front of her, blocking her view.

It was busy in Cambridge. The weather must have brought people outside. They flitted around Florence in their bright summer outfits like newly emerged butterflies, some darting quickly past, others crowding the pavement and staring at the college buildings behind her, their camera phones held aloft. She looked to her right, where a building jutted out into the street, shaped like a turret with arched balcony windows that glinted in the sun. She couldn't see through the glass but she imagined that inside were study rooms furnished with bookshelves, writing desks and old chairs made from carved wood and soft, worn leather. She imagined patches of sunlight on wooden floors that creaked under foot and a smell like a second-hand book-shop. She pictured the writer Sylvia Plath sitting at a desk by the window composing 'Mad Girl's Love Song', a poem Florence had read just a week ago. She pictured her clos-ing her eyes and imagining the world was dead, as she'd described in the poem, then opening them and looking for that feeling that the world was reborn again. Wishing the person she loved would return. Florence could imagine just how Sylvia Plath had felt writing that.

Florence closed her eyes and the imaginary Sylvia Plath, the people on the street, and thoughts of Howard and her parents and tomorrow all disappeared. When she opened them again Jasper was standing in front of her. She jolted in surprise, blushing at the irony.

He looked concerned. 'Are you okay? What did your parents say? Are you alright to come?'

'Yeah, it's fine.'

He smiled with relief and held his hand out to help her off the wall. 'Let's get going then, before you have a change of heart.'

She put her hand in his and dropped down to the pavement. Her legs felt as though she'd just got off a fairground ride.

Andrew was walking over to join them, his phone to his ear, the other hand swinging a carrier bag. Wilf was following behind, frowning at his mobile again.

Andrew got off the phone then stopped and stared straight ahead. 'Oh my goodness.'

Florence looked at him, puzzled.

'What's up?' Jasper said.

'Oh wow.' Andrew was gaping now, like he couldn't believe what he was seeing.

Florence and Jasper turned to see what he was staring at.

The crowd of people standing in front of the wall taking pictures of the college had grown since they'd arrived.

Florence noticed that on the lawn in front of the college there was a small group of people fussing around a man who looked vaguely familiar.

'Hey,' Jasper pointed in their direction. 'Isn't he that astronaut? The one who sang that song?'

'Commander Chris Hadfield.' Andrew snapped out of his reverie and wrestled off his rucksack, dropping it on the path and frantically rummaging through it before pulling out his iPad. He handed it to Florence. 'Take a photo for me.' Without waiting for an answer he pushed his way through the milling crowd and clumsily scrambled over the wall.

'Oh shit,' Wilf said. 'What's he doing?'

They watched, incredulous, as Andrew approached the Commander then stopped in front of him, his long arms making erratic, angular shapes as he talked with his hands.

'Oh God,' Wilf said. 'He's gonna make a total fan boy of himself. You think we should stop him?'

'No way!' Jasper was watching with amusement. 'Andrew loves that guy. Have you ever seen him this excited?'

Florence took a couple of pictures.

Wilf watched, unimpressed. 'You realise he's going to talk about this all the way to Wales, now. You remember what he was like when he got a retweet from Brian Cox? He'll drive us all mad. And he's making a proper arse of himself.

I mean, look at the poor guy's face. Andrew's definitely pissing him off.'

Florence looked at Wilf doubtfully.

'We should drag him away before they call security or something.' Wilf made like he was going to go and fetch him but then Andrew started walking back across the grass towards them.

Florence had never seen him smile so widely. His hand was flapping at his side and he kept looking behind as though he was reluctant to go. When he re-joined them he continued to stare at the man in awe.

'Happy?' Wilf snapped at him. 'I mean, do you think we might be able to get on and get going now?'

Andrew didn't seem to hear him. 'That is one of the most exciting things that's ever happened to me.'

'That's great, Andrew, I'm really excited for you, but Wilf's right, we ought to make a move,' Florence said. 'We've got a long way to go.'

'Yes, Howard ... You're right. We should go.'

Florence turned away from the college and felt something brush against her, knocking her sideways. She looked up and saw a cyclist weaving past her, cycling one-handed as he swung a rucksack up onto his shoulder.

'Watch it,' Jasper shouted, taking Florence by the elbow to steady her. 'Are you okay?'

'Yeah.' She stared after the cyclist as he swerved around a bollard, making a woman and child jump out of the way. Something had caught her eye. Something familiar. She stared harder at his bag. Swinging from the zip of the front pocket was a round, orange reflector. She gasped and scanned the pavement frantically.

'What's up?' Jasper said.

'That man.' She looked up just as the cyclist disappeared around a corner. 'He's taken Andrew's bag!'

ULTIMATE QUESTION: ZOMBIE APOCALYPSE, WHAT'S YOUR STRATEGY ...?

FLORENCE: Oh, I'd hide in the woods, find some abandoned cottage, grow stuff, just generally not draw attention to myself ...

JASPER: Would you also make friends with seven tiny diamond miners?

ANDREW: Wouldn't you feel duty-bound to help humankind and find a solution? A vaccine for example?

FLORENCE: I'd probably be a bit too busy protecting my family and my vegetable patch.

JASPER: I think I'd start a community, build a fortress, and recreate life as it was but simpler.

WILF: Wow, you're a bunch of domestic sitting ducks. Where's your bloodlust? There are millions of rotting, rabid corpses taking over the world and you guys are playing house? I wouldn't be letting them get away with it. I'd be out there hunting them down. Kicking as much rotten arse as I could find.

ANDREW: Aren't you supposed to aim for their head? You really need to cause substantial structural damage to a zombie's brain if you want to kill it.

WILF: Oh, you bet I would. I'd get myself a crossbow and I'd take those suckers down one after another, like Daryl in *The Walking Dead*.

ANDREW: The flaw in your plan is you have to get your arrows back and they'd be covered in zombie brains. Knowing you, you'd wipe them on your jeans. I'd get myself a tiger. They're the ultimate hunters. If you had a tiger you could train it to kill so that you wouldn't have to get your hands dirty.

WILF: Where's the fun in that? I'd rather kill them with my bare hands.

ANDREW: That's because you like violence.

WILF: Yeah, well, you just like cats.

ANDREW: I do. I like cats a lot.

Chapter Eight

They ran down the crowded street.

Wilf was in the lead, his eyes fixed ahead as though he was locked on target. He was running with a determination that reminded Florence of the robot in *Terminator 2*.

Jasper was managing to stay close behind Wilf. He wasn't a natural runner but he was more agile than Wilf, making him quicker at weaving through the slow-moving pedestrians.

Andrew and Florence were bringing up the rear, Florence struggling to keep hold of the remaining bags and not drop Andrew's iPad.

She knew she didn't have a hope of keeping up with them but she was still racing as fast as she could, fearing Wilf might catch the cyclist and unleash a rage that would make the situation a whole lot worse.

They turned a corner. Wilf and Jasper had stopped and were standing in the middle of a crossroads, panting heavily and looking in all directions.

Florence swore under breath, scanning the street. There were people and bikes everywhere, fighting for road space with buses and taxis. On the pavement a queue at an ice cream vendor mingled with a queue at a bus stop. Several people were looking at them curiously.

'We've lost him,' Jasper confirmed.

Wilf made a noise like an angry dog and balled his fist, hitting it against a lamppost. It clanged loudly, drawing more attention from the crowds around them.

'What was in your bag, Andrew? Anything important?' Jasper said.

He shrugged. 'No, not really. Just my phone, my money, my keys, that sort of thing.'

Wilf gawped at him. 'What do you mean not important? That's, like, *everything* that's important.'

'No, I still have my iPad and I left my laptop in the van. I've even got my shopping.' He held up a carrier bag that contained the toothbrushes, some toothpaste and packet of wet wipes.

'My purse was in your bag,' Florence said. 'I don't have any money now.'

'Oh. I'm sorry, Florence.' He looked worried for a moment then brightened when he saw that she was holding his iPad. 'Hey, did you get a good photo of me with Chris Hadfield?'

Jasper looked at him, incredulous. 'Andrew, don't you think you should be a bit more bothered? You've just been robbed. You should call the police at least.'

'Maybe.' His eyes were fixed on his iPad screen. 'I doubt they'd be able to do much though, and besides, I can't. I no longer have my phone.'

Wilf took his own phone out of his pocket and pressed it firmly against Andrew's chest.

'Alright, alright.' He passed his iPad back to Florence and dialled the number. When he started to talk he turned away from them and paced the pavement.

Florence sighed and Jasper dipped his head to study her face. 'Are you okay?'

'Yeah, I just feel like an idiot. It's my fault. I should have been watching Andrew's bag. That guy took it from right under my nose.'

'Don't be daft. No one expects to get robbed like that and we were all there. Don't blame yourself.' He put a brief, comforting hand on her shoulder.

Florence felt suddenly electrified. When he took his hand away she could still feel the warmth and weight of it. She imagined it still there.

A pair of fingers clicked in front of her face. Andrew was flapping his hand at her impatiently, still holding the phone to his ear. 'Notebook and pen,' he said in a hushed voice. 'You always have a notebook and pen.'

'Oh, sure.' She rummaged in her bag and took them out, folding the pad over to a clean page.

Andrew leaned against a wall and made some notes. When he finished he hung up and turned back to the others.

'They've alerted patrol cars to look out for anyone fitting the description of the cyclist and they're going to get someone to review CCTV footage from the street next week.'

'Next week?' Wilf looked aghast. 'What the fuck is wrong with them? No wonder people pull this shit.'

Jasper shrugged. 'What else can they do?'

'They can get off their arses and start taking these scumbags off the street, that's what they can do. I'm sick of it. It happens all the time where I live. Druggies and pond-life nicking anything not chained up. You can't leave anything in our workshop without someone thinking it's up for grabs. It's a joke. They know they'll get away with it so they basically do what they like. They're taking the piss.'

Andrew cast his eyes to the ground and shifted uncomfortably. He hated it when Wilf was angry.

Florence watched Wilf curiously. Despite his undisguised rage she found his sense of morality reassuring.

Andrew held the pad out to her, careful not to catch Wilf's eye. 'I've written down the crime number in case you want to use your parents' insurance for the purse.'

'Oh, hey, it's not worth it. It was a tenner and some loose change and the purse was an old one anyway. It's not worth the hassle, really.' Especially as it would involve explaining where she was to her parents, she thought.

'I guess there's nothing else we can do then,' Jasper said. 'Perhaps we should get moving?'

'But what about money? Me and Andrew don't have

any now. Can we afford it? Petrol and food and stuff? Obviously I'll pay my share when I get home if you've got enough, Wilf?'

For the first time the reality of the situation seemed to dawn on Andrew and he looked worried. 'Oh, please, Wilf, I've got plenty of money at home. I can pay for petrol and everything when we get back. If you haven't got enough I could always phone my parents.'

'No,' Wilf said, pushing himself away from the wall. 'Don't call them. The tank in the van's full and I don't think we'll starve. Let's just get out of here before anything else happens.' He started walking.

Florence hung behind and apologised to Andrew. She couldn't shake the feeling that she'd messed up. Again.

Andrew seemed genuinely unbothered. 'Why are you apologising? You didn't take my bag.'

The phone in Andrew's hand rang and he looked momentarily startled.

Florence gestured for him to answer it. 'Maybe that's the police calling back.'

Wilf tutted. 'Yeah right, they'll have filed his case under Don't Give a—'

'No, this is Andrew, but I'm with Wilf,' Andrew was saying.

Wilf stopped and turned around.

'Yes, we're in Cambridge but we're leaving soon. We're going to Wales.'

'Give me that.' Wilf lunged for the phone but Andrew instinctively ducked out the way.

'Uh huh, yes the country of Wales. No, Borth y Castell. A village on the west coast. Um, no, we're looking for someone.'

Wilf got him in a headlock but Andrew continued to talk. 'Geographically speaking it's really quite ... Wilf, get off!'

Wilf finally grabbed his phone back and immediately hung up.

Andrew smoothed out his T-shirt, flustered. 'What did you do that for?'

'I didn't give you my phone so you can spill my private business to anyone who asks.'

'Sorry, but I didn't tell him we were going to find Howard or anything. What does it matter?'

'It just does, alright? Who was it? My brother?' He pressed a button to see his call history and frowned.

'He said he was your brother's friend.'

'Mitch doesn't have friends. None worth talking to anyway.' He turned the phone off and put it back in his pocket. 'You don't touch my phone again, alright? And don't go telling anyone else where we're going.'

Andrew nodded and Wilf started walking again, his pace much faster now.

Jasper fell into step with Florence and leaned towards her, his voice lowered. 'Something tells me Wilf might not have told his brother he was taking the van today.'

Chapter Nine

Wilf was in a mood.

It didn't make much difference. He was never the most upbeat person, but he was definitely brooding, Florence thought. He drove silently, his jaw set as he concentrated on the road ahead. He was impatient, tutting at the traffic lights and other drivers as though they were conspiring to slow him down, and the way he was changing gear reminded Florence of the way her mum prepared vegetables when she was mad at her dad and biting her tongue, all firm, angry efficiency. Florence never asked her mum what was wrong and she wasn't about to ask Wilf. It was obvious that the morning's events hadn't helped but his mood had been aggravated by Andrew.

When they'd got back to the van Andrew had proceeded to hop into the passenger's seat and programme Wilf's sat nav.

'Er. What are you doing? I can do that myself,' Wilf said.

'Yes, but you won't do it right. You've set it to use motor-ways. I don't travel on motorways.'

Wilf looked momentarily unsure whether he was being wound up but Andrew's face told him otherwise. 'Andrew, we're going from one side of the country to another, how can you possibly expect me to avoid motorways?'

'It really doesn't make that much difference. I've checked. It only adds fifty-six minutes to the journey but actually it'll probably save us time because we're less likely to be stuck in a traffic jam or get mown down by a lorry driver with sleep apnoea. We want to get there safely, don't we?'

Wilf was staring at him with his mouth open.

Andrew scanned the floor and Florence and Jasper exchanged a look, ready to brace themselves for an outburst, but instead Wilf sighed heavily and sat down, slamming the door behind him. 'Get in the back and don't get in here again, *comprendez*?'

Andrew quickly removed himself and Wilf started the engine, his lips a thin, tense line.

As they made their way out of Cambridge and headed west, Andrew settled back into his good mood. He talked quickly, reeling off everything he knew about Chris Hadfield, as though in his excitement he felt the need to purge himself of information whether anyone was listening or not. As he talked he uploaded the photo Florence had taken onto his laptop, cropping it so there was no one else in the shot and adjusting the lighting until he was happy enough to make it his screen saver. 'What do you think?' He turned the screen around so that Jasper and Florence could see.

The picture showed Andrew in mid-sentence, his mouth open and his arms aloft. The commander was looking at him with an expression of concern.

'I still can't believe you went right up to him like that,' Jasper said. 'What did you say?'

'Oh, you know, just that I was a big fan of his work. His space travel, of course, not his singing, and that he's probably one of my top five favourite astronauts of all time.'

Wilf gave a sarcastic snort. 'Wow, I bet he was equally thrilled to meet you.'

Andrew ignored him. 'He asked if I was going to the talk he's giving tonight in the students' union so I told him I'm not a student yet but hopefully when I am he'll come back, because, even though I'll be studying particle physics, I am fascinated by space travel and I wish I was brave enough to want to be an astronaut.'

'Ah, what did he say to that?' Florence asked.

'He said that if I challenged my perceptions I could be brave enough to do anything.'

'Nice,' Jasper said, nodding thoughtfully.

'I know, but then I told him that would be pointless because my mum has already told me I'm not allowed to go to space because it's dangerous and too far.'

'Oh man.' Wilf covered his face with his hand. 'You are so deeply uncool.'

'I don't care. I've just met one of the most famous astronauts in the universe and he's now following me on Twitter.' He swivelled his laptop back towards him and started humming the chorus of David Bowie's 'Space Oddity'.

'He's happy,' Jasper said to Florence.

'Yeah, that's good.' Florence was sitting with her feet up on the chair, her notebook resting against her knees.

Jasper looked at it. 'What are you writing about, anyway?'

She closed her notepad, immediately self-conscious. 'Oh, you know. Not much. Just doodling.'

'Doodling words.' He gave her an amused look. 'Isn't that called writing? Are you sure you're not a closet journalist taking notes on us all? Maybe you're like that woman you were talking about, who went into those mental institutions and spied on everyone.' He waved his finger at her, eyes teasing. 'I always thought you seemed too normal for Manor Lane.'

Florence smiled but could feel the beginnings of a blush appearing on her face. This was the point when she should say what she'd actually been doing but she'd never be able to explain without sounding weird. The last words she'd written were 'super massive black hole' and 'Gonville and Caius', the last being the name of a college she'd seen on a Cambridge street sign. To Florence they were letters and sounds in perfect arrangement. Like flavours that were made for each other, the blend of spices in a really good curry or the delicious layers in a tiramisu. She wanted to capture them the way people might take a photo of an attractive building or a beautiful sunrise. Unfortunately she'd learnt pretty early on in life that it wasn't an interest many people understood. You only needed a few of your friends to look at you like you're weird to realise some things were best kept to yourself.

'Yeah, that's what I'm doing. Spying on you all.' She put her notebook back in her bag. 'And I'm coming to the conclusion that we're all surprisingly normal.'

'You're right, you know. I never really felt normal till I came to Manor Lane.'

'Me too, but what about when we're not in Manor Lane?'

He shrugged. 'I feel normal right now.'

'Then maybe normal is just a state of mind?'

'Or maybe normal is everything and everything is normal?'

'You've totally just expanded the definition of normal.'

'I always thought it should be more inclusive.'

'Normal is conforming to a set of averages,' Andrew said in a voice of mild irritation. 'You can't just change the definition of a word.'

'Maybe definitions can be subjective.'

Andrew looked dumbfounded and Jasper held up his hands in defeat. 'Okay, you win, but the words "conforming" and "average" aren't exactly selling it to me.'

Florence actually really liked the word average. It sounded relaxing. She pictured it in her mind like a landscape of low grassy hills. She wanted to write it down. She wanted to capture the entire conversation. She clicked her pen automatically and Jasper looked back at her.

'You *are* making notes on us.'

'No.' It sounded like a lie.

'Can I see?'

'No!'

He just smiled at her. 'If you write a novel one day can I be in it?'

'I'm not a writer.'

'Of course you are. You're never without a pen and a notebook.'

Florence put the pen down on the table, feeling silly. 'I'm not. Not really.' Writing words in a notebook made her about as much of a writer as being an art lover and collector made a person a painter. 'I like words and language, that's all. I don't know what I want to be really.' The truth was she hadn't thought about it for a long time. Years ago she'd read *Little Women* and imagined herself as Jo, making up stories and immersing herself in her love of words. A few years later she started to realise she experienced them differently to other people. Sometimes they just made her feel something: pleasure, disgust, calm, intrigued. Sometimes they formed shapes, patterns, colours. Sometimes they were clear enough to form objects or scenes. Nouns were the most confusing because the words in her head didn't fit their definition. Brick was a fist. Flower looked like cotton wool. Paper was shiny. When you said things like that out loud you tended to get looked at strangely. There were sniggers in the classroom. People thought you were making it up. After a while Florence learned to keep her words to herself. She stopped creating and started collecting instead. Sharing was no longer an option. If she didn't experience words like other people did, how could she possibly write for them?

She swallowed hard, wanting to think about something else. 'What about you, Jasper? What would you like to be?'

'Hmm.' He slouched in his chair and stroked his chin, his head to one side. He looked like he had several options and was weighing them up. Picking a favourite.

'It sounds kind of corny but I'd like to help people. Sometimes I think I'd like Howard's job. Most of the time I think I'd like to be a teacher.'

'Oh.' Florence hadn't been expecting him to say that. He was a born performer. 'Why a teacher?'

'I dunno.' He sat forward again, his focus back on her. 'Have you ever had a teacher who's inspired you?'

'Um.' She'd taken so much time off school in the last year she could hardly remember her teachers. The occasional times they'd ventured away from the curriculum and talked to her as an individual it was usually with the same looks of concern or frustration that her parents would give her. The only inspiring teachers she could conjure in her mind were characters in books and films. 'Not really.'

'Just a person then. Someone who's said something that's

inspired you, or made you feel like you can do more than you'd given yourself credit for?'

That was an easier question to answer. 'Howard.'

'Exactly.' He brightened. 'Howard always knows what to say, he takes us seriously, he encourages us to be braver. That's inspiring. My drama teacher's the same. If it weren't for him I'd still be hiding at the back, wishing I had the courage to be the one in the spotlight. He made me feel like I could get up there and do it. I guess I just appreciate those moments. Those people. I want to be able to do that, if I can, because I know how important it is.' He gave a self-deprecating laugh. 'They'll probably just hate me though.'

Florence couldn't imagine that ever being the case.

'Don't be a teacher, mate.' Wilf was looking at him in the rear-view mirror, the engine idling as they waited in traffic. 'They'll crucify you. Kids are evil. Fact. They wind teachers up to the point of breakdown and then the teachers take their miserable lives out on the kids. The whole system is a vicious, never-ending dog fight.'

'Wow. Okay.' Jasper gave Florence a look that said, *what's up with him?* 'Maybe you just didn't have the right teachers?'

'You got that right.'

'Hey!' Andrew called out suddenly. He was looking up from his laptop in disbelief.

'What's up?' Jasper said.

'Wilf! I said I didn't do motorways.'

90

Wilf fixed his gaze ahead. 'Dude, I'm just following a short diversion.'

Andrew stood up, his expression part angry, part panicked. 'But, I gave you a route.'

The van crept forward with the traffic then Wilf braked suddenly, making Andrew stumble forward.

He steadied himself by holding onto the side of the van. When he looked out of the window he did a double-take. 'Wilf!'

'How the fuck did you know where we were anyway? You were on your laptop the whole time!'

'It's called GPS, Wilf. I'm following the van on my laptop.'

'Right. 'Course you are, coz that's totally normal!'

Andrew was frantically gathering his things and stuffing them in his carrier bag.

'Andrew, calm down,' Jasper said. 'It's not that big a deal. I'm sure Wilf will get off at the nearest exit, won't you, Wilf?'

'For fuck's sake. What difference does it make? This is way quicker. At least it would have been if it wasn't for that jack-knifed lorry and all those morons slowing down to rubberneck it.'

Andrew was breathing hard. He swung the strap of his laptop bag onto his shoulder.

Florence stood up, attempting to take his arm and calm him down but he turned away and reached for the back doors.

'Andrew, don't.' Jasper jumped up but Andrew had

already swung the door open, just as Wilf edged the van forward again.

Andrew swung out into the road with a panicked yelp, gripping the door handle. There was a skid of tyres as the car following the van had to break hard to avoid hitting the swinging door. Andrew's bag slid from his shoulder and his arms were shaking from exertion. He dropped down into the road.

'Andrew, get back inside,' Jasper shouted, reaching out of the doors for him. A car beeped.

'What the fuck is he doing?' Wilf shouted.

Andrew looked around at the three lanes of queuing traffic, all facing him, then saw the grass bank at the side of the road and took off towards it.

'Hey!' Jasper watched in disbelief then turned to the others. 'I'll go after him. Get off at the nearest exit and come and find us. I've got my phone.' He jumped down onto the road and shut the doors behind him.

Florence looked out of the side window but a lorry nudged forward in the outside lane and blocked her view.

Wilf hit the steering wheel with both hands. 'I knew this was a bad idea. He's a bloody nut job. If something happens to him it's not my fault. If he ends up under a lorry it'll bloody well serve him right.'

Florence moved to the sofa and sat down so she could see out of the front windscreen. There were blue flashing lights in the distance and the cars in front were being directed into a single lane. 'Do you know how far it is to the exit?'

Wilf stabbed at the sat nav screen several times. 'About five miles once we get past this accident. Not far.'

'Right, so if we get off there hopefully Jasper will have found him and we can go and pick them up.'

Florence had seen enough of Andrew's meltdowns at Manor Lane to know that they didn't last long. He'd become distraught and irrational and have to go and sit somewhere on his own, but then he'd come to terms with whatever had set him off balance and he'd think of a way past it. Some compromise which made him feel that the problem had been solved. Keeping Wilf calm enough not to set Andrew off again, that was going to be the real problem. So long as they didn't lose him it would be fine. Florence tried to slow her breathing and stay positive. Her phone buzzed and she took it out of her pocket. It was a text from Jasper. It read: *Sorry guys. He's gone!*

Florence's notebook

The definition of normal

ADJECTIVE

1. Conforming to a standard; regular, typical or expected.

   'My normal college hours are nine to five.'

   'It is normal to feel upset upon receiving bad news.'

   1.1 A person free from mental and physical health disorders.

   'They had a normal, healthy baby.'

   'She often wondered what it was like to be a normal, functioning human being.'

NOUN

1. The usual, expected, typical state or amount.

   'Normal service will resume shortly ...'

URBAN (favourite answer)

1. A word inapplicable to human beings.

FLORENCE

1. Round, smooth and bumpy like a cobbled street.

Chapter Ten

The half an hour it took to get off the motorway felt more like two hours to Florence. She kept her phone in her hand, watching the screen for text updates from Jasper. As time went on they became punctuated with starred swear words and elaborate suggestions on what they might do when they finally tracked him down.

Once they managed to pull off the motorway Wilf back-tracked down a road which ran parallel to it.

Jasper texted to say he was waiting somewhere by the entrance to a farmhouse so Florence knelt on the seat with her eyes fixed on the road ahead, looking out for them both.

The road was little used with no markings and long, thick grass blurring its edge. The few houses nearby were set well back from the road and some distance apart. Between them, vast empty fields rose to a gentle range of hills in the distance. Only the trees that marked the edges of the fields broke up the view. Andrew could be anywhere, Florence thought nervously. If he sat down in any one of those fields the grass was so long it would hide him completely. He'd stay stubbornly silent if they called him. He wouldn't think to stay visible or consider what would happen if he couldn't be found. She looked back at the road and was relieved to see Jasper step out in front of them.

Wilf braked hard and pulled into a lay-by, his tyres skidding on the gravel and kicking up a cloud of dust.

Jasper was holding his hands up to show he'd had no luck.

Florence slid the side door open and stepped out to join him. The air was stiflingly warm and she could hear the low rumble of the motorway nearby.

'No joy,' Jasper confirmed. He rubbed the back of his neck and looked across the field, weighing up the possibilities. 'I've not gone far. The motorway is just behind those trees. When he runs off at Manor Lane he usually sits under the tree on the front lawn so I figured he'd do something similar.

Florence looked at the row of thin, sparse trees on a hump at the other side of the field. Behind them was a tatty looking farmhouse with a collection of outbuildings facing each other in a courtyard. The buildings looked derelict, with crumbling brick walls, rotten wooden doors and patched tin roofs. Between the buildings were piles of rusted machinery and tyres. The only sign of life was the occasional fat red hen, picking its way around the debris and cooing softly.

Florence pointed in its direction. 'Did you try over there?'

Jasper shook his head. 'I thought he'd probably go sit under a tree. He wouldn't go where there might be people.'

'Yeah, but it doesn't look like anyone's around. Just animals, and he likes animals. I think he actually prefers them to people.' She remembered Andrew saying goodbye to his cat with more feeling than he showed his parents.

'That's true.' Wilf slammed the van door shut and locked it. 'He feeds the pigeons at lunchtime like those mad bag ladies in Eaton Park. He'll be over there somewhere, sitting in a huddle and telling the chickens a tale of woe.'

Wilf was right. Andrew was sitting slouched and deflated on a grassy mound behind a barely standing, single storey shed. His chin was rested on his arms, which were folded on his knees, and he was watching a chicken peck at the grass just a few feet in front of him. He looked up, startled, as the others came into view nearby, then he wiped at his face and looked away.

Florence realised he'd been crying and hesitated, wondering whether it might be better to give him some time alone. At Manor Lane this sort of thing happened a lot. She'd got used to the emotional outbursts, the tears and swearing and toppled furniture. She was used to other people handling it and staying out of the way while trained staff calmly followed procedure. She never got involved. She didn't need to.

She wondered what Howard would do.

When Florence first arrived at Manor Lane she'd spent

the first three days sitting on the floor of the cloakroom, trying to make herself as small as the bags on the floor. She probably looked just like Andrew did right now, except she hadn't cried. Crying would have meant she felt something and back then Florence felt almost nothing at all. Everything had been an effort: feeling, talking, eating, thinking, being . . . She just wanted to be left alone.

The staff took it in turns to try and engage her in conversation but soon started leaving her to it, probably expecting she'd get bored eventually and come out, curious. She'd get told when it was lunchtime, when her parents were in for a meeting, when they were having lessons and every other punctuation in the day, but they didn't push her to join in.

On the third day, just after lunch, she stretched out of her ball and repositioned herself so she could lean against a soft, padded coat on the bench.

Something caught her eye. There was a book trapped behind the leg of the bench in front of her. It looked well worn and was facing away from her so she couldn't see the title. There was a picture of a lizard on the back cover.

She stared at it for a while, annoyed that it had caught her attention, then curiosity got the better of her and she leaned forward to retrieve it, sitting back in her huddle before she turned it over in her hands. *Holes* by Louis Sachar. She'd heard of it. She'd even looked for it in the library once but all their copies had been checked out. She scanned the back cover blurb, not reading it, just absorbing the shapes and patterns of the letters, and it was at that moment that she heard the soft squeak of Howard's shoes approaching in the corridor.

'If only, if only,' Howard said in a loud, humorous voice as he passed, without seeming to look at Florence at all.

She hadn't realised he'd been quoting from the book until she happened upon the sentence later that day.

When Howard joined her on the floor the following day to ask how the book was going, she told him she'd actually taken it home and finished it and was now reading it a second time. It was the start of the conversation she'd been resisting.

As she stood on the grass, staring at Andrew, who was hanging his head as Wilf ranted angrily and Jasper tried to placate him, it occurred to her for the first time that maybe it was Howard who had left the book behind the bench in the first place.

'Don't shout at him.' Florence put a hand on Wilf's gesticulating arm. 'It won't help.'

'Well sorry, Florence. Forgive me if I'm a little annoyed that we've driven halfway across the country to find Howard and now he wants to arse everything up just because I drove on a road with more than two lanes in it. If he had any money on him I'd go find Howard myself and leave him to fork out for a very expensive cab ride home but as he's also managed to mess that up it seems like I'm stuck with the job of getting him back in my van.'

'I'm not going back in your van.' Andrew shook his head

firmly. 'Nuh uh. I can't trust you now.' He was rhythmically picking the grass then dropping it in a neat pile near his feet.

Wilf looked at Florence and Jasper as though imploring them to understand why he would soon be resorting to violence.

'You're supposed to be my friend,' Andrew continued.

Wilf flung his hands in the air and made a gesture that suggested he was speechless.

'He is your friend,' Jasper said firmly. 'We all are.'

Andrew sniffed and wiped his nose on his sleeve. 'Why don't you take me seriously then?'

Wilf was pacing. 'Oh, believe me, I take you very seriously, Andrew.'

'Not how I feel about things. You think that I'm autistic so that means I don't care about stuff but I do. All I've ever wanted is to have friends like everyone else. Friends I can trust not to laugh at me or treat me like I'm nothing.'

Wilf looked like he was going to argue but Andrew continued.

'At school the only kind of friends I made were the sort who'd talk about a party and invite me but then give me the wrong address on purpose. Friends who'd do things to wind me up so they could watch me get in trouble. Friends who'd write swear words in my notes and change my name to Android in the school paper just before it got sent to the printers.'

Wilf made a noise like a snort then quickly cleared his throat.

Andrew stared at him angrily. 'It's not funny. You think I'm just one big joke but it's not funny to me. You call me names and put me down but I'm not a robot. I do care. I spend a lot of time trying to understand people because I want them to like me. I don't want to annoy people or say the wrong thing. I really am trying, but I feel like I'm always failing and disappointing people. Why does no one ever try to understand me?' He coughed several times in quick succession then blinked hard and looked away.

Florence felt her eyes prick with sudden tears. She hadn't realised Andrew felt like that. He'd get angry or stressed if things didn't go the way he wanted but she'd never seen him cry before. She felt bad that she hadn't realised just how much he wanted to be liked and how much it hurt him to feel like he wasn't.

She was tempted to go and take his hand but she knew he didn't like to be touched. Instead she walked over and sat down on the grass beside him, her back to Wilf.

'Andrew, we're here with you now because we care about you. We're all your friends. Even Wilf.' She turned back to Wilf and narrowed her eyes, daring him to contradict her.

Wilf held up his hands in surrender.

'Thank you, Florence.' Andrew gave a small smile of gratitude, still watching the chickens.

She watched them too for a while then said, 'Okay, here's an ultimate question for you. What came first, the chicken or the egg?'

He answered without even pausing to think. 'The shell can only be made by a protein found in the ovaries of a chicken and so the chicken had to be around first to make the egg.'

'Oh. So, where did the chicken come from then?'

'It evolved.'

'That's weird. Why's everyone been arguing about it all this time then?'

'It's kind of a new theory.'

'Maybe we should put the word out.'

He cast a sidelong look at her, as though suspecting she was mocking him. 'I think people enjoy the paradox.'

'Yeah. You're probably right.'

They returned to their silence and Jasper joined them on the grass.

Wilf sighed, defeated. 'Alright, alright. I'm sorry, okay? Andrew, I really didn't mean to upset you. I didn't realise it was that big a deal. I should have taken you more seriously and I will next time. I give you my word that I won't drive on another motorway all the way to Wales and back.' He put a hand on his chest and looked earnest.

Andrew gave him a brief, dubious glance.

Wilf slumped to the ground beside them. 'You know what I'm like. I'm like it with everyone. I take the piss and give it some banter. I don't mean anything by it. If I call you a name it probably means I like you.' He started picking at the grass too, only he threw the shredded blades in the direction of the chicken. 'I know what it's like to have people assume things about you that aren't fair or true. I've had it all my life. As soon as anybody found out I was a Connor kid they'd have me written off as some kind of waster. Everyone's heard of my brother. He's always in trouble, my cousins too. If ever there was trouble at school people always assumed it was my fault. I must have started it. Or if I couldn't keep up with the work it was because I was lazy or stupid. It's like, as soon as people know you've got problems it's all they see. They don't take the time to find out what you're really about.'

'Yeah, I get that,' Florence said. 'People are either scared of talking to me or they're asking if I'm okay all the time, like I might just crack up in front of them. Even my own parents. No one treats me like a normal person any more. I can see it in their faces when they talk to me. They're thinking, *you're that depressed girl*. It's all they see.'

'It's true. People have taken the piss out of me for years,' Jasper said. 'Guys aren't allowed to get anxious about stuff, are they? They're supposed to be tough. *Man up* and all that. Guys with eating disorders can't be taken seriously. They see an anxious guy with an eating disorder who takes drama and they either laugh at me or assume I'm gay.'

Wilf looked genuinely surprised. 'I thought you were gay.'

Jasper gave a brief, world-weary laugh. 'Yeah, cheers, Wilf.'

Wilf continued to look sceptical. 'C'mon, you're a total Ian McKellen fan.'

'He was Gandalf, dude! Look, it's not like it should even matter. I just don't see why people have to make assumptions about me, or use it as a put down. They don't take the time to get to know what I'm really like. You three probably know me better than some of the so-called friends I've spent years at college with.'

Wilf nodded in agreement and concentrated hard on the grass.

'Well, I never thought Jasper was gay,' Andrew said seriously. 'It's obvious from the way he is around Florence.'

Florence felt like the air had been sucked out of her. Her mouth dropped open but no sound came out.

Wilf burst out laughing and said with genuine affection, 'Andrew, you're so priceless.'

Jasper rolled his eyes as though he was tolerating a couple of young children.

'Alright, enough,' Florence snapped, standing up and irritably brushing the dried bits of grass off the back of her jeans. 'I don't know about you but I want to get on and find Howard.'

'Yeah, come on.' Wilf got up slowly. 'You coming, Andrew?'

Andrew looked at Wilf then nodded. 'So long as you stick to your promise.'

'I always keep my word. Just let me stop at the services first. I'm gonna need a sugar and caffeine fix to get me through the rest of this journey.'

They walked back to the van, Andrew and Wilf already sniping at each other again.

'Are you sure people don't just assume you're a waster because you hit people and get excluded from schools?'

'Are you sure people don't just assume you're a robot because on car journeys you malfunction when someone deviates from the approved road type?'

Jasper grinned and looked at Florence for the first time since Andrew had made his embarrassing comment. 'Business as usual then.'

'Yeah,' she said, but she wasn't really listening. Instead she was thinking about what Andrew had said, and remembering how hard Wilf had laughed.

Ultimate Question:
Date Night Deal Breakers ...

ANDREW: I don't like dates.

WILF: Have you ever been on a date?

ANDREW: No.

WILF: Why not?

ANDREW: Because I don't want a girlfriend, or a boyfriend, and because people go on dates to get to know each other better, which means I won't know them well enough to be sure they won't do something I don't like.

WILF: Like what?

ANDREW: Like eat with their mouth open, or talk too much, or laugh really loud, or wear jewellery that makes a jangling noise or too much make-up or really strong perfume, or touch my plate or my food or me when I'm not expecting it, or talk about really stupid, pointless things like pop music or reality TV or *Star Trek: Voyager.*

WILF: Right. There's your deal breakers.

ANDREW: Surely everybody hates those things.

WILF: They're not everybody's deal breakers, Andrew.

ANDREW: So what would yours be?

WILF: Easy. Vegetarians, vegans, dungarees.

FLORENCE: You can't not like a girl because she doesn't eat meat.

WILF: I never said I wouldn't like them. I just wouldn't date them. I like all food. I like cooking food. I like experimenting and sharing. We're social creatures. Food is sexy. It's like this shared, physical language. If I'm going to date someone we need to be talking the same language, or how are we ever going to connect with each other?

FLORENCE: When you put it like that, it almost sounds romantic.

WILF: And, as for dungarees, if you want to look like a Mario brother then you're on your own, love.

JASPER: I like vegetarians and vegans and dungarees can be really cute. In fact most of the things on Andrew's list wouldn't really bother me. I just like girls who are nice and kind of pretty in a natural way and say thank you to waiters and laugh at my jokes.

FLORENCE: You sound like you'd date a lot of girls.

JASPER: No, not true, they'd have to be special. I'm just not sure I could describe what constitutes special. It's not something I can put into words. What about you?

FLORENCE: Yeah, I guess I know what you mean. Maybe I just like guys who are interesting to talk to. Who don't call women 'love' and are attracted to who they are not what they look like. Decent guys with a hint of special.

ANDREW: Florence likes Spider-Man.

Chapter Eleven

There was a welcome blast of cool air as they walked into the services. It was busy, and there was a cluster of people milling in the lobby, waiting for friends and family members by the toilets near the entrance. The drone of a hand dryer kept switching from loud to muffled as people went in and out, the doors banging behind them. Andrew muttered something about 'the necessary evils of the public bathroom' and walked off towards them, while Wilf headed straight for the newsagent's.

'Ooh, gift shop,' Jasper said, with a childish playfulness and started towards it. He looked back, gesturing for Florence to follow him.

She obliged willingly, glad to have a distraction.

The only person in the shop was a member of staff not much older than them. She had an elfin face and cropped pink hair and was flicking through a newspaper as though she was only interested in the pictures. She didn't look up when they walked in.

Jasper said hello anyway then wandered up the aisle humming to a terrible soft jazz version of a Taylor Swift song playing in the background.

Florence picked up a snow globe and turned it upside down, watching white flakes gently settle on the spire of Coventry Cathedral.

Jasper inspected a large novelty rubber that looked like a twenty-pound note and sniffed it, frowning.

Florence gave an involuntary laugh. 'What were you expecting it to smell of?'

He dropped it and pretended to look sheepish. 'Okay, now I feel silly.'

Florence turned a carousel of teddy bears wearing T-shirts with names on and looked for theirs. She could only find Andrew. It had huge feet and a narrow face, its expression hangdog. She turned around to show it to Jasper.

He was wearing a sock monkey hat and pulling the same majestic expression he'd used when imitating Morgan Freeman.

'I like it,' Florence said, mirroring his serious expression.

He picked up a white fluffy hat with black panda ears and tossed it towards her.

She put it on and continued to browse.

Jasper appraised her with undisguised affection. 'You look adorable. Can I stroke your ears?'

She laughed self-consciously, her cheeks colouring.

'Too soon?'

She opened her mouth and searched for something to say but there were no words. She had no point of reference for a situation where a guy in a comedy hat, who made her feel as though she was teetering on the brink of something uncertain and scary, asked if he could stroke her anything.

He gave her that slightly charming, teasing, flirting smile that always left her tongue-tied and sweaty-palmed. She knew it wasn't real flirting. Jasper could turn on the charm with anyone. She'd seen him do it many times before: to the nursing staff, to Aggie the cook and even to the casual cleaning staff who spoke little English yet understood enough to greet him like an old friend. He charmed visiting professionals and parents in for meetings, and a few weeks ago he had Dennis Fairchild's little sister following him around like a star-struck super-fan. Jasper flirted with everyone. He probably didn't even realise he was doing it. When she reminded herself of this her heart would slow down and that familiar sense of hopeless resignation would return.

'Are you planning on buying those?' a sullen voice enquired. The girl with the pink hair was looking at them from behind the counter, her head cocked to one side as she eyed them with weary disdain.

'I don't know, what do you think? Does it suit me?' He strode over to the counter and leant on it, looking up at the girl and posed comically.

She couldn't help but laugh.

Yep. Resistance really is futile, Florence thought. She

took her hat off, feeling suddenly foolish. It was too hot to be wearing anything furry. 'We ought to find the others. They'll think we've done a runner.'

'You're right.' He pulled the hat off and rearranged his hair then raised his hand in farewell at the girl behind the counter.

Andrew was waiting in the lobby. He was ticking slightly, coughing and pulling at the neck of his top, his eyes cast down as though not wanting to be noticed.

'Where were you?' he said when they approached. He held up his wrist and showed them his watch. 'It's one o'clock. I have lunch at one o'clock, but my lunch was in my bag and my bag was stolen.'

'Oh right, of course.' Jasper looked around at the café. 'You want me to buy you something? I've still got my mum's twenty quid. We can sort it out next week.'

Andrew nodded but didn't look at him.

Florence cast around for Wilf and saw him on the pavement outside. He was talking on his mobile, his head bent and his mouth up close to the handset. He looked as though he was angrily spitting out his words, his free hand jabbing the air like he was poking an invisible person in the chest.

'I'll text Wilf and let him know where we are,' she said, not wanting to disturb him, then followed Jasper and Andrew to the café.

'Florence, would you like anything?' Jasper asked as they stood in the queue.

Andrew picked a packet of plain cheese sandwiches out of a chiller, inspected them suspiciously then put them on a tray.

Florence tried not to look at them. 'Oh, hey, don't worry about me. You should have something though.'

Jasper was also avoiding looking at the food. 'I'm alright. I'm just going to have a tea, maybe some chocolate. I've got enough money if you want something though, honestly.' He looked at her and smiled, encouragingly. 'Go on, let me treat you. What would you like? A sandwich? Cake?' He looked up at the board behind the counter. 'An all-day-Mega-Grill breakfast?'

'I'll just have the same as you, if that's okay.'

He frowned at her, concerned it wasn't enough, and she looked back at him innocently, challenging him to say it.

Jasper would live on tea and chocolate alone if he had his way. They were the only things Florence had ever seen him willingly eat or drink without being watched by Manor Lane staff.

When Jasper had first arrived he never ate his meals in the dining room with the rest of them. Instead he'd have them later, in a room with just him and two members of staff. Sometimes Florence would hear shouting, a fist on a table, a clatter of a plate or the slam of a door as he walked out in protest.

In the last few weeks he'd joined the others for mealtimes. The staff hung around as they usually did but one of them was always paying close attention to Jasper.

He'd pick at his food begrudgingly and push his plate

away after eating only the bare minimum, getting up to leave as soon as he was allowed. He hardly ever said anything. His expression was resigned and his body slouched. After he left the room he'd instantly return to his usual self: cheerful and jocular and pacing with pent-up energy.

On Jasper's second day at Manor Lane, Wilf had made a typically inappropriate comment about the calories in the chocolate bar Jasper was eating. Jasper countered it by pointing out that he wasn't actually anorexic. Instead he described himself as 'a bit fussy' and said with what sounded like false bravado that he 'functioned better on an empty stomach'.

Florence soon figured out that Jasper's real problem was anxiety. He was running high on adrenaline, like a car being revved in neutral. Avoiding food was one of his ways of managing it. He'd got used to eating less and a habit had set in. Now eating would cause him to react as though he was being confronted with a phobia. Florence found it hard to watch him struggle to fight it. She'd try to avoid catching his eye when they were sitting at the dining table but in her head she was cheering him on, the way you might cheer on a patient in physio attempting to walk again. She just wanted him to be okay.

'Are you sure I can't get you something else? I don't want you to be hungry.' He saw her eyes flick back to Andrew's sandwich. 'You're sure you don't want one of those?'

'It's fine, honestly, I'll have what you're having,' she repeated.

He frowned at her and then at Andrew's sandwich then he took another packet out of the chiller. 'How about we share?'

'Sure.' She felt a jolt of surprise but fought to keep her face neutral. The fact that he was prepared to eat something so she wouldn't go hungry gave her a sudden lump in her throat. 'Thanks.'

They sat at a table, Jasper teasing his sandwich into tiny morsels which he ate slowly, chewing more than necessary and swallowing like he was forcing it down.

Florence pretended not to notice and kept talking instead. She babbled about Andrew meeting Chris Hadfield and how good it was to get out of the house and how much she liked Cambridge and that it was true what people said about a change of scenery, even when it was only a motorway services near Coventry, and even though she was worried about Howard she was glad they were all out together like this, doing something away from Manor Lane and home. She could hear the words coming out of her mouth like insubstantial froth. A voice in her head was telling her to *chill out and shut up* but the words kept coming, making her start to wonder whether she was high. Was that possible? Was she reacting to something she'd eaten or the caffeine she'd drunk?

Jasper gave up on his sandwich and Florence stopped talking as quickly as she'd started. She was nervous, she realised. Trying too hard. Trying to distract him so he'd relax and eat.

'You alright?' He had an amused expression on his face as he picked up his mug of tea.

'Yeah.' She gave him an apologetic smile. 'I think I might be experiencing my first caffeine rush. Three cups in one morning is a new one for me.'

'It's actually called theine when it's in tea, not caffeine,' Andrew said without looking up from his laptop. 'Same molecule. Different effect.'

Florence wrinkled her nose. She didn't like the word *theine* nearly as much.

'Well, whatever it is it's doing you good,' Jasper said. 'I think you've said more today than you have in a week at Manor Lane.'

'Oh.' She looked down at the table.

'No, don't look like that.' He nudged her foot. 'It's a good thing. Remember when I first met you? You didn't speak for days.'

She felt a twinge of embarrassment. She didn't like to be reminded about how she'd been. In her twelve weeks at Manor Lane she'd come a long way. Fortunately Jasper hadn't seen her when she first arrived. When she was switched off and just wanted to be left alone. At that point she didn't communicate, she rarely washed her hair or changed her clothes, she didn't taste the food that was put in front of her. What was the point?

Over the following weeks at Manor Lane things began to change. CBT, hours of conversations with Howard, enforced routine, yoga and meditation, meeting other people like herself, who didn't fit in and probably never would. They started to have an effect. She started feeling things again, remembering herself, wanting to join in more. She'd find herself talking, asking questions, wanting to know things. She sometimes even caught a glimpse of a feeling, an intense feeling like excitement, passion or joy, and it was like the sudden burst of a firework. A brief and unexpected flash of colour and life that would quickly vanish and leave her wondering where it had come from and hoping it would come back. She was remembering who she was and the things she liked. She was slowly becoming a person again, but she wasn't fully formed and solid yet. She was an apparition, and sometimes she worried if she looked too hard she might vanish again.

She gave him a tentative smile, deliberately not looking at the last piece of sandwich on his plate. 'I think we've all come a long way.'

'We've actually come one hundred and forty-two point five miles,' Andrew said. 'We're not even halfway yet.' He put the rest of his sandwich in his mouth and chewed thoughtfully.

A sudden, loud banging on the window made all three of them jump and turn around.

Wilf was standing on the pavement outside, gesturing towards the van. His usually pale face was flushed pink and beaded with sweat. 'Come on!' he mouthed with exaggerated impatience.

Jasper observed him with casual interest. 'He's particularly tense today, don't you think?'

Florence hadn't even sat down before Wilf swung the van out of the car park, forcing her to grab hold of the door to steady herself. She looked out of the side window, watching as they turned onto the main road. Two men on motorbikes turned in as they left. The man in front was wearing a bandana instead of a helmet and his black leather jacket had a faded pair of white wings painted on the back. A woman about to cross the road with a little girl had to quickly scoop her up and step back onto the pavement to get out of his way. Florence felt her stomach swoop as she watched the scene and she stayed by the window, not wanting look away until the woman and the little girl had safely crossed the road.

Chapter Twelve

Andrew's laptop slid precariously from his knee. He stopped typing and repositioned it, frowning. 'You're going a little fast.'

'I'm doing thirty in a thirty limit,' Wilf snapped. 'You want to check that on your GPS?'

'You're supposed to slow down for corners.'

'You can't even see the corners so how can you possibly ju—' Wilf gripped the steering wheel harder and glanced irritably at the rear-view mirror. 'If you don't like the way I'm cornering you should have let me drive on a nice straight road like, er, what's that thing called? A MOTORWAY!'

'There's no need to raise your voice.'

'I am not. Discussing. My driving with you. Any more. Do you understand? If you complain again, you'll walk to Wales. If you criticise me again, you'll limp. Got it?'

The van swerved left and Andrew, Jasper and Florence moved involuntarily with it. Andrew looked as though he was about to protest but he swallowed his words and tugged at the collar of his T-shirt instead.

Jasper caught Florence's eye, gestured to Wilf with an incline of his head and raised a questioning eyebrow.

Florence answered with a similarly puzzled look. Wilf being tetchy wasn't surprising but up until then his driving had been unremarkable. Florence considered all the times her mum had snapped at her dad when he was driving too fast, telling him that the sign of a good driver was forgetting you were being driven. According to this rule Wilf had gone from good to terrible in the space of a visit to the motorway services.

She checked her watch. It was two o'clock. They didn't have a schedule. Even Andrew had given in to the idea that so long as they arrived before it got dark it didn't make much difference. There was no need to rush.

The van lurched again and the road surface changed. The rumbling sound of tyres grew louder and their seats vibrated. The contents of the van rattled and a camping kettle slid off the little cupboard opposite Andrew and landed at his feet. He looked up, alarmed, then his eyes narrowed. 'Where are we?'

'I thought you were following the van on your GPS?' Jasper said.

'I was. The road ran out.' He stood up, carefully placing his laptop on the chair, and stooped to look out of the side window. There was a thud as the van hit a pothole

120

then swung violently, throwing Florence forward against the table.

Andrew stumbled towards the opposite window. 'Oh!'

The van came to a sudden, noisy halt.

Florence looked out of the front window to see where they were but could only see a cloud of dust rising from the ground.

'You okay?' Jasper said to her.

'Yeah.' She rubbed her elbow. 'What's going on?'

Wilf was already out of the van. He'd left the driver's door wide open.

Florence and Jasper looked at each other curiously then jumped up to join him.

They were parked next to three towering stacks of hay made up of round flat bales piled on top of each other. They must have been fifteen feet high and each had blue tarpaulin wrapped around its base. There was the occasional rush of sound as a car passed by on the road they'd just left but other than that the only sounds they could hear were the rustling of dry grass in the breeze and the persistent chirping of crickets.

Florence stepped down from the van and tried to get her bearings. They had exited the road on a short, dirt track then Wilf had ditched the van behind the hay. The van was parked on what looked like the old foundations of a house or farm building. There was a half-demolished wall on one side and a pile of spare tyres beside it. They were surrounded by fields and hedgerows. A heat shimmer rose in the distance, blurring the horizon.

'Wilf, what are you doing?' Andrew called out from the van.

There was a 'Shhh' from the other side of the hay stacks then Wilf ducked back into sight.

'What's going on?' Jasper asked him.

Wilf just waved his hands as if to say *not now* then peered back around the hay.

The urgency in his body language made them all fall silent.

Florence could hear the faint, low rumble of an engine, gradually getting louder. She stayed hidden, looking through a gap in the haystacks to the road they'd just left.

Two bikers came into sight. They were sitting low with their arms wide on their handlebars. Together they took up both lanes of the road and were travelling fast. The engine noise grew to a roar, vibrating the air around them, then it faded quickly as they continued over the brow of a hill. An uncomfortable sense of foreboding took over as Florence realised she'd seen these men before.

When the sound of chirping crickets could once again be heard Andrew came out of the van, his expression a mixture of confusion and alarm. 'You were hiding from them. Why were you hiding? Do you know them?'

Wilf was slumped with his back against the haystack, his eyes closed. At the sound of Andrew's questions he suddenly snapped back to life. He opened his eyes, let out a cry of frustration, then turned and started to hit the hay repeatedly, as if it were a punch bag.

Andrew shifted on his feet and cast his eyes to the ground.

Jasper's concern slowly turned to curiosity. He walked around the haystack and stood back, taking in the scene. 'It's a Minion. Wilf, you're punching a Minion.'

Florence followed him, confused, then saw that the three tall towers of hay had been decorated to look like giant Minion characters from the animated film. They had white painted tyres for eyes and black spray-painted smiles. The blue tarpaulin wrapped around the bottom of each had an extra section pinned to the front to make it look like the bib of a pair of blue dungarees, and propped up between them was a large plywood sign with PYO STRAWBERRIES TURN LEFT IN 500 YARDS painted in large red letters. The Minion on the right had only one eye and Wilf appeared to be punching it hard in the side.

Jasper shook his head thoughtfully. 'Never a dull moment.'

Wilf continued to rage against the straw.

Florence thought about the bikers almost running over the little girl crossing the road and bit her lip. She had a feeling this was more serious than Jasper realised.

When Wilf paused to catch his breath Jasper seized the moment to attempt to make light of the situation. 'Mate. Whatever's wrong I don't think taking it out on Dave is going to help.' He turned back to Florence. 'Is that Dave? The one-eyed one?'

Florence looked at the haystack again and shrugged. 'I dunno. It might be Kevin.'

'It's not funny.' Wilf took one last swing at the haystack. The sign advertising the strawberry picking slipped on one side then fell to the ground with a clatter.

Wilf stopped and put his hands on his hips. He was panting and sweating heavily.

'Is it your brother?' Jasper said. 'Is it because you took the van?'

'But you said he let you borrow the van?' Andrew said.

Wilf sat down on the edge of the concrete foundations and wiped his forehead with his arm. 'I said he'd probably let me, and any other weekend he might have. I didn't know ... Shit.'

'What?' Jasper said. 'What's the problem?'

Andrew was blinking rapidly and pacing. 'Does your brother have plans? Was he going somewhere?'

'Oh yeah, Mitch had plans, only I've gone and arsed that up for him apparently, and now they're after me. Those guys on the bikes. We've got something they want.'

Andrew shook his head, agitated. 'We've got something? What does that mean? I don't understand.'

'What is it, Wilf?' Jasper said. 'What have you got that they want? Why are they looking for us?'

Wilf ran his hand through his hair then sat down on the

ground with a heavy sigh. 'Apparently Mitch left a stash in the van. I swear I didn't know. I've not seen it. He says he hid it there last night and was planning on selling it today. He's got people waiting for it. They got twitchy, and now his dealer has sent some of his guys to fetch it.'

Andrew stopped pacing and gasped. 'Are you talking about drugs? Do you have drugs in your van? Why? Why would you bring something like that?'

'I told you, I didn't do it on purpose. I had no idea it was in there till Mitch kept calling, asking where the van was.'

Andrew twitched like he was trying to escape from his T-shirt. 'This is not good, Wilf. This is really not good.'

'Yeah, well, tell me about it. Like I said, we're not a regular kind of family, are we? Mitch has been doing all sorts of shit for years. Weed at first, then coke. Now people sell it for him. They meet in the pub round the corner from our house. I could tell something was going on this weekend, that's why I wanted out of it. I hate this shit. I don't want anything to do with it, but it's like trouble follows me. I can't escape it.'

He folded his arms around his knees then rested his head on them.

Florence felt a pang of sympathy for him. He looked scared. Usually he was the scary one. 'Can't we just return it?' she said. 'Tell your brother you'll be back tomorrow? Or hand it over to those guys? That's all they want, right? They won't do anything to you if they get it back.'

Andrew shook his head like a disapproving parent.

She thought about it. If they passed it on did that make them accessories? Were they already? It sounded more serious than a few roll ups or some drinks bought with fake ID.

'What else can we do though?' she said. 'If we take it to the police, they'll arrest Wilf's brother. There'll be repercussions, surely, but what other options are there?'

'Could we just dump it? You know, leave it in a field or flush it down a toilet or something?' Jasper said.

'But then what if those guys are waiting for us in Wales?' Florence said. 'Andrew told them the name of the village we're going to. If we've dumped their stuff what'll they do to us then?' She couldn't help but look at the bruise on Jasper's cheek and imagine how much worse it could have been.

Jasper winced as though he could feel her eyes on him. 'She's right. Maybe our only option is to make like we don't know it's there, avoid the bikers, do our thing and return the van tomorrow. Then whatever happens afterwards is nothing to do with us.'

Wilf had been staring into the distance. He was zoned out, as though he was looking at something that wasn't there. His breathing quickened, his mouth became a thin line, then he stood up with his fists balled at his sides.

'I'm done with this. I'm not having it any more.'

'What are you doing?' Jasper tried to catch his arm but Wilf was already striding in the direction of the van.

The others followed.

He flung open the back doors and paused, assessing the

cabin for a moment, then he climbed in and started grabbing at anything he could get his hands on, tossing it aside then quickly moving on. He rummaged through the little cupboard and sent saucepans and plates clattering to the floor then he toppled fishing tackle and upended a box of camping equipment. He straightened up and hit the side panels of the van so they clanged like steel drums then collapsed the table and unfolded the bed, looking under the thin cushion which doubled as a mattress. He unzipped it, feeling around inside before tossing it to the floor with its cover half off and the foam inside exposed.

Jasper followed him around the van, trying to stop him by talking calmly and pulling him back but Wilf just threw him off. Florence tried to surreptitiously tidy up behind him, picking up the fishing gear and leaning it back behind the chair, placing a frying pan back on its hook and returning the plastic plates and bowls to the cupboard under the stove.

When the cupboard door wouldn't close she pushed the plates back further and there was a clatter as something fell. She knelt down to get a better look and saw that the back of the cupboard had come away and fallen against the pans. She tried to prop it back up but something was in the way. She felt behind it and her fingers closed on something smooth and soft. It felt like plastic. She pulled it out. It was a clear food bag full of white powder.

'Um, Wilf?'

'Is that it?' Jasper crouched down behind her, looking over her shoulder.

'I guess.' She could feel her heart beating faster. Just holding it in her hands felt weird. She'd never seen drugs like this before. Marijuana, a bit. Some paraphernalia at the few parties she'd been to before but nothing like this. This was on a different scale. People made films about this stuff. People went to prison. Died. She wondered what her mum would say if she could see her now. She'd have a class A fit for sure. She'd look at her with hurt disappointment and say that line, 'but you were always so good, Florence. So sensible,' as though she couldn't work out how she'd turned out to be so very different.

'There's not that much of it, is there?'

Wilf was staring at it curiously too. 'It's two grand's worth, Mitch said.'

Jasper whistled. 'Two grand, just for that.' He bent down and looked at it closely.

Florence held it away from them as though they could breathe it in through the plastic.

'You know what's funny?' Andrew was standing outside the van, shifting from one foot to another. 'Coca-Cola used to have cocaine in it but then they took it out. They took it out but they left the sugar in, and the irony is sugar is more addictive.'

Jasper wrinkled his nose up. 'Give me a sugar high any day. Brain chemistry's a delicate thing. Why would anyone want to mess with that?'

Wilf snatched the package out of Florence's hand and

jumped out of the van. He positioned himself like a shot putter and, with a cry of rage and effort, launched it into the air. It arced gracefully then landed with a soft thud in the grass. A small white puff of powder rose from it and hung in the air.

Wilf stared angrily at it, his chest rising and falling fast, then his face crumpled, he sat down on the ledge of the van and started to cry.

Ultimate Question:
Favourite Dunking Biscuit?

WILF: Oh, man alive that really is the ultimate question.

ANDREW: I don't like dunking biscuits. You get bits
in your tea.

JASPER: Not with a KitKat. Two fingers, don't dunk too long,
and don't break them.

WILF: Mate, I don't think you should choose a biscuit with
chocolate on the outside, they can't take the heat.

JASPER: I have to have chocolate; it's my drug of choice.

WILF: Well, you should at least go for a chocolate chip, that
way the biscuit offers some heat protection.

JASPER: You're taking this very seriously, Wilf. You haven't
said what yours would be yet?

WILF: Don't rush me.

FLORENCE: I love Jaffa Cakes.

WILF: They're not a biscuit. They're a cake. The clue's in the name, duh.

ANDREW: Wilf is actually correct.

FLORENCE: So what does that make Kendal Mint Cake?

JASPER: Or spotted dick.

WILF: For fuck's sake, guys if you can't take this seriously . . .

FLORENCE: Alright, I'll go for a Fruit Shortcake then. Sweet and a bit fruity.

ANDREW: Raisins look like flies.

JASPER: Andrew, I think you should pick a biscuit.

ANDREW: Can I have it next to my cup of tea but not dunk?

JASPER: Fine.

ANDREW: Alright then, maybe a shortbread. Rich, plain, no bits.

WILF: Good choice, they dunk well.

ANDREW: I TOLD YOU, I DON'T DUNK.

JASPER: Jeez, this is almost as tense as the Doctor Who debate. Wilf, you're going to have to pick one.

WILF: Shit. Alright. A Hobnob. No chocolate. Tough, thick, gritty.

JASPER: I knew it. It's our biscuit choices that define us . . .

FLORENCE: Hey!

Chapter Thirteen

Andrew walked away, twisting a section of hair at the back of his head and Florence and Jasper exchanged a look of panic.

Wilf never cried. Not like this. Not in a vulnerable way, limp and noisy as if he'd given up caring. She was used to seeing tears of rage prick in his eyes, his face red and wild, his temper defying you to feel sorry for him. That was easier to deal with. This was real sadness. This needed someone who knew what they were doing. It needed Howard to spirit Wilf away to his office, only to have him leave an hour and a half later with a headache and a lot to think about. She looked around as though expecting a member of staff to come out of nowhere and take control but there was no one there to do it for them. She wanted to do something useful – make tea, fetch biscuits, like she'd done at Jasper's house.

She carefully stepped nearer, as if he were a stray dog she couldn't predict. 'Hey, it's okay.'

'No, it's not okay. It's shit. My life's shit.'

'I know.' She grimaced. 'I mean, obviously I'm sure it's not, but I mean I know how you feel. We've all felt like that.'

'No, you don't know. I'm trapped. I'm stuck with it. I can't go back but I've got no choice.'

'There's got to be options, Wilf. There'll be a way.' She looked at Jasper to back her up but he was looking like he knew exactly what Wilf meant. He was in the same boat, stuck with a home life he wouldn't choose for himself.

It wasn't fair.

'I'm going to end up just like him.' Wilf sobbed and choked then twisted his face so he could wipe his eyes on the sleeve of his T-shirt.

Jasper shook his head firmly. 'You won't. You just launched an expensive bag of drugs into a field. Would your brother do that? You're better than him. You're ...' He searched for the right word. 'You're decent.'

Wilf gave a hollow laugh. 'I'm not talking about Mitch. I'm talking about my dad. Working in that shitty garage in that shithole place. Every day the same. No wonder he's miserable all the time. That's my future. It's all I'm good for.' His voice was muffled and breaking. He coughed and sniffed and wiped at his eyes with the back of his hand.

'I thought you liked your dad?' Florence said.

He shrugged like it didn't matter. 'I do. That's why it's so hard. Ever since mum left he's just ... He's given up. He used to be fun to be around. We'd go fishing, we'd do stuff together. Now he just works. He can't afford not to.

134

When he's at home he just sits in front of the telly. I make him dinner but he gets back so late he eats alone, if he can be bothered to eat at all. It's like he's switched off. He can't handle Mitch and all this shit he keeps bringing to our door. If I left how would he cope?' He stooped to pick up a stone and launched it at the spot on the grass where the package had disappeared then he sat down again, his shoulders slumped. 'I hate this.'

Jasper put his hands in his pockets and paced in front of him, kicking at stones as he considered Wilf's problem. 'You can't live your life to make someone else happy though. He wouldn't want that. No one would want that.'

Wilf shook his head sadly. 'It's too hard to do anything else.'

Jasper nodded reluctantly. He knew how that felt too.

'What do you want to do then, Wilf? What would make you happy?' Florence remembered that Howard had asked her the same thing once.

He shook his head and exhaled noisily. He didn't want to play that game. He didn't want to be talked into a positive frame of mind.

They stayed silent, letting the question hang in the air. That awful word, Florence thought, floating out of reach again, then Wilf looked up. He swallowed hard and rubbed his eyes with the back of his hand.

'This is what I like. Being outdoors.' He'd stopped crying but his face was blotchy and his voice flat. 'Not in a garage, fixing engines all day. Not in a college. Not anywhere that stays the same, with the same boring four walls, day after day. When I'm in the garage all I want to do is get in one of those bloody cars and drive somewhere.'

'Where would you go?'

'Anywhere. Somewhere with a view, I suppose. Maybe by a lake or a river. I'd catch a fish. Cook it for dinner.' He nodded as he conjured the image in his mind. 'It's cooking that I really like, you know. Proper cooking. Not the poxy, fiddly sort that's so tiny and pretentious it could disappear up its own arse, but real food. Simple, quality stuff. Steak and burgers and slow-cooked pork, handmade buns and sauces, that sort of thing. I saw a bloke once, at a farmer's market in Norfolk. It was the last time I went fishing with my dad. We pulled over so he could use their toilet. He didn't want to buy any food, said it all looked overpriced and poncey. He wanted to stop at a hotdog van in a lay-by. Anyway, this bloke I saw was cooking chilli and selling it out the side of a converted H van. Vintage, bright red. It looked the business. He was cooking on this big pan on the counter. It was like street theatre. The smell of his food was unbelievable. The queue went right round the car park. That's the kind of job I want. So perfect it's not even a job, you know what I mean? Pitching up in a van and making food people want to queue for. I'd give anything to do something like that.'

'Sounds good, Wilf.' Florence didn't know what an H van

was but she still had a picture in her mind. 'I can imagine you doing that.'

'Yeah well, that sort of thing doesn't happen to me.' He ground his foot into the dirt. 'You know, Mitch took me to a school fair once. I must have only been seven or eight years old. It was just before I got excluded the first time. There was a competition. You paid 50p to pick a place on a map where there might be treasure hidden. The teacher felt sorry for me cos I didn't have any money so he let me have a free go. I chose Great Yarmouth because I'd been there with Dad once. We'd had fish and chips on the sea front. My kind of treasure. The next day they announced the winner in assembly. I'd won a bright red truck, all boxed and shiny. I took it home and showed Dad but he didn't believe I'd won it. I got a smack round the head and he took it straight back up to the school. The teachers must've put him straight but I never saw the van again.' He stared at the long grass and sighed heavily. 'Even my own dad didn't believe anything good could ever happen to me.'

'You deserve to be happy though, Wilf. Everyone does. You have to grab your chances.' She was quoting Howard again, and although she wasn't saying it with the same authority she believed it this time. Things were easier to believe, she realised, when you said them to someone else.

'Yeah well, there's no point thinking about it, I have no chances. I should know that by now. I'm just being stupid.'

'No. You're not being stupid,' Florence insisted. 'You *have* to do what you want to do. You're clever, Wilf. You can already drive, you can cook, you can fix stuff – like the way you fixed Jasper's door. You've got skills and principles ... You're like seventeen going on twenty-seven. Honestly, Wilf. I wish I could do half those things.'

He sniffed and swallowed hard, managing a smile. 'Thanks,' he said eventually. 'You know, if you fancy me you should have just said so.'

She smiled and punched him lightly on the shoulder. 'Don't be a dick.'

'So, what are we going to do?' Andrew said. 'Are we just going to leave that here?' He was looking at the patch of grass where the package had landed with a troubled expression. 'Because ...'

'We'll have to. It's not coming with us and I'm not giving it to them. If they find us I might tell them where to look.' Wilf got up and walked resolutely back to the van.

Jasper rubbed his chin and contemplated it too. 'I s'pose they'll be more interested in finding their stuff than giving us any trouble.' He looked from Andrew to Florence, as though checking they agreed with him.

None of them looked convinced but then the engine roared into life and they had no choice but to hurry back into the van.

The more miles they covered the more the sombre mood started to lift. Andrew was navigating from his laptop, guiding Wilf down the smaller roads where they were less likely to be seen. Florence stopped looking out of the windows whenever there was a roar of engine noise and the bikers became less of a threat and more just another surreal incident in a day that was turning out to be more eventful than her entire stay at Manor Lane.

Wilf had turned on the radio and Andrew was wearing his noise cancelling headphones.

Florence and Jasper made small talk while building towers using a pack of cards Jasper had found in the drawer of the little table. When Wilf took a sharp left and Jasper's three-tier pyramid collapsed again he gave up and suggested he teach Florence how to play poker.

'You want to join in, Andrew?' Jasper waved to get his attention and pointed to the cards.

Andrew took his headphones off and looked quizzical.

'Poker. You want to play? We're gambling for matches.' He tapped the box he'd found hidden in Wilf's camping equipment.

Andrew wrinkled his nose. 'Not really.'

'Come on, mate. I thought you'd like an opportunity to use your mathematical brain.'

He wrinkled his nose. 'Brains are hardly a requirement. It's a game of chance. Card distribution is the deciding factor.'

Florence watched Jasper's hands as he deftly shuffled the cards, fanning and dovetailing them before presenting them to Florence and instructing her to 'cut the pack'.

'You look like you've done this a lot.'

'My mum taught me when I was eight. I used to play with the guys in the pub when she was singing.' He trapped a matchstick between his teeth like a gangster chewing a toothpick.

'Why am I starting to feel like I've got no chance?'

Andrew snorted, not looking up. 'Perhaps because you don't have much grasp of the laws of probability. Wilf, you need to take a left turn at the T-junction, and you might want to brake a little sooner this time.'

Wilf turned the radio up before indicating and Andrew put his headphones back on.

'So, what was it like hanging out in bars and watching your mum sing?' Florence tried and failed to imagine her own mum doing anything nearly as flamboyant. A second cup of coffee in a department store café was about as wild as it got whenever they went anywhere.

He dealt out two cards each and pulled a face. 'Not great. I mean, don't get me wrong, I thought she was glamorous in those days. Sparkly dresses and lots of make-up and her singing voice is good, but then you get a bit older and you realise your mum's in a barely there dress, dancing like she's on MTV and being chatted up by blokes with beer froth in their beards.' He flashed Florence a half smile then he picked up his cards and studied them. 'It's no wonder I need therapy.'

'You got any pictures of your mum, Jasper?' Wilf said, looking in the rear-view mirror.

'Piss off, Wilf.' Jasper launched a matchstick at him without looking up.

'You get on with her though, don't you?' Florence remembered some of the times he'd mentioned her before. His descriptions made her sound unpredictable but fun, someone he felt more responsible for than was normal but still cared a lot about.

'Hmm.' His face darkened momentarily then he tapped the table impatiently. 'Look at your cards then, Florence. Let's see how lucky you are.'

There was a song playing on the radio and Jasper was singing along. Wind was buffeting between the open windows and Florence was enjoying the occasional blast of a welcome, cooling breeze. It ruffled her hair, pulling tendrils out of her ponytail and whipping them across her face but she didn't push them away; she liked that they helped mask her expressions. She was trying hard to perfect her poker face but it wasn't the cards she needed it for. Every time Jasper made her laugh, or caught her eye when he sung a meaningful line in a song, or spread his hands on the table so that the tips of his fingers were almost touching hers, she felt such a strong physical reaction to him that she was sure he must have noticed. Her heart was racing as though they'd been playing a sport and a film of sweat had formed on her skin. All she could think about was how much she wanted to reach out and touch him.

'One more?' He shuffled the cards again. 'I'll play properly this time, stop letting you win.' He grinned at her and suddenly she wanted to get out of the van and take a deep breath.

'In a bit, maybe.' She stood up and stretched and moved to the side window, leaning her face into the wind. She let the rush of air fill her ears and cool her face and reached her hand outside as though trying to catch hold of it.

They'd crossed the border into Wales a short while ago and the countryside already looked different. The colours were more vibrant; it was greener, prettier, emptier. The road followed a stream that meandered through a field, sparkling where it pooled on a bend before passing under a small stone bridge. She wanted to get out and run beside it, burn off some of the adrenaline that'd been building in her all day.

Jasper got up and leaned out of the window on the other side. He took a deep breath and closed his eyes, the wind messing up his hair. The song changed to something soulful and slow and he hummed along.

Florence smiled to herself. The river disappeared around a bend and they passed a row of tiny stone cottages and a corner shop. They both sang the chorus, quietly at first, then more confidently. She sang at the people as they passed, at the cars in a petrol station and the two motorbikes pulling out of the forecourt. Her breath caught in her mouth and she ducked her head back into the van. 'Oh shit.'

'What's up?'

She flattened herself against the side of the van. 'Those bikers. I've just seen them. I practically waved at them.'

Jasper crossed to her side and leaned out of the window to look at the road behind. 'You're right. We've got company.'

She tried to pull him back. 'Get in!'

He didn't move. 'Florence, there's a giant bulldog wearing a pair of headphones sprayed on the back of the van. Your arm and my face are not going to be what gives us away.'

Wilf accelerated and Andrew flipped his headphones off, irritated. 'What now?'

'Sorry, Andrew, you're just going to have to put up with my driving for now.' Wilf watched his side mirror as he took a corner without slowing down.

Andrew let out a cry of indignation and Jasper took Florence's elbow, steering her back to her seat before the van lurched again.

Chapter Fourteen

The van rattled and clattered as it bounced over a speed-bump. A box of Wilf's belongings slid backwards and then sideways on the floor as he sped up and took a corner. Florence stared ahead at the narrow road, willing it to be free of traffic. The few people on the footpath were looking with a mixture of alarm and disapproval at the noise and speed of the vehicle.

There was a lorry making a delivery outside a bakery and Wilf swerved around it, forcing an oncoming car to brake hard. It beeped long and loud.

A man who'd just stepped onto a pedestrian crossing jumped back and shouted something incoherent.

Andrew frowned and whimpered but kept his eyes fixed on his laptop. 'You should take the next left.'

'What? It's a little side road.'

'You don't want to stay on this road. If you keep going you'll get to a railway crossing. It's too risky. If the barrier's down they'll catch us up.'

Wilf made a sharp left and they drove under an arched railway bridge. Seconds later the sound of the motorbikes behind them became amplified and more threatening.

Coming out of the bridge they were greeted by an idyllic country view. A green field to the left and a hill rising steeply to the right. Wilf sped up and the sound of the motorbikes grew quieter as he put some distance between them. They followed the road around the bend of a hill then Wilf suddenly slammed on the brakes. 'Shit!'

There was a sheep standing in the middle of the road. It was looking at the approaching van with docile indifference.

Wilf swerved sharply and they bumped onto the grass. There was a scrape of metal against wood as it clipped a signpost.

Andrew gasped. 'What are you doing?'

'What do you think I'm doing?' Wilf snapped, his voice bordering on hysterical. 'I'm trashing my brother's van for the sake of saving a dumb ass sheep on the road. You think I actually wanted to do that?' He hit the steering wheel with both hands. 'Shit! I really am dead now. I may as well pull over and let them finish me off.' He swung the van back on the road.

Andrew looked panicked. 'Don't do that.'

'You got any other bright ideas? They. Are. Not. Going. Away'

The noise of the engines was now so loud it sounded like they'd been surrounded but Florence didn't dare look out the window.

145

Several loud thuds resounded, making them recoil. Someone was thumping against the side of the van.

'Next left,' Andrew called out. 'It looks like there's a ford. You might lose them there.'

Wilf made the turn then took a sharp intake of breath as he saw it ahead. 'That's a river, Andrew!'

Florence and Jasper both looked out of the front windscreen. Between a row of trees ahead was a glimmer of fast moving water.

Andrew was tapping frantically on his laptop. 'It's marked as a ford. You can cross it.'

'Don't be insane. If water gets in the air intake we're screwed.'

'Deep water roads dot com says it's a well maintained ford with a concrete base, twelve inches deep at the most and fifteen feet across.' Andrew blinked rapidly as he read.

'It's just flowing fast,' Jasper said, looking over Florence's shoulder. 'I reckon you can make that.'

'We'll have to now, we've got no choice.' Wilf gripped the steering wheel harder and sped up.

The road sloped down on the approach to the ford and as they hit the surface of the water it arched away from them on all sides, the crash of water momentarily drowning out the revving engine.

Jasper and Florence gripped the table as the van tipped to one side. It felt like it was being pushed by the force of the stream.

Florence held her breath as though it was her that had just been plunged under water.

Seconds later the van sped up and the water level receded as they started to climb out.

Wilf checked his side mirror. 'They can't cross. It's too deep for them.'

Florence exhaled and put a hand to her thumping chest.

They drove out the other side and up the lane then Wilf stopped at the top, the engine idling. He closed his eyes, his arms rigid and still gripping the steering wheel. When he opened his eyes he checked the mirror then sprang into action, throwing open the van door and jumping out.

'Hey, what're you doing? Keep going!' Andrew clutched his laptop and gathered his belongings to him as if he were about to be robbed for a second time that day.

Jasper peered through the side window. 'It's fine. They're stuck.'

Jasper slid the door back and stepped out.

Florence followed cautiously.

The two men were pulled up on the other side of the water, engines revving.

'Come on then,' Wilf shouted, walking up to the edge and splaying his arms wide like a football player taunting the opposition.

They cut their engines and one of them dismounted.

Wilf dropped his arms and backed away but his chin was

147

still raised and defiant. 'You want your stash?' He gestured at the van.

The biker with the bandana put his hands on his hips and stared Wilf down. 'Don't mess us around. Get it, now.'

His mate was assessing the rapid flowing water as though deciding whether he could wade across and throttle Wilf with his bare hands.

'It's not here.' Wilf pointed into the distance. 'It's behind you.'

The biker almost looked around then fixed his eyes on Wilf again. 'Seriously. You go get it and you throw it over here, or we'll be coming for you.'

'No can do. It's in a field off the A470. I chucked it in a field behind a row of giant straw minions.'

The second biker looked at his mate then. 'I know where he means. I saw them. They've got these tyres for eyes and . . . ' He made a gesture that looked like he was miming a large pair of glasses.

His mate stared at him, irritated, then looked back at Wilf. 'How do I know you're telling the truth?'

'Well, I don't want it, do I? I don't need this grief. Ask my brother. I've never wanted anything to do with it. I didn't even know it was in the van till you two turned up. I just want to hang out with my friends and have you guys as far away from us as possible. My brother's business is his business and I want him, and you, and that,' he pointed back to where they'd come from, 'to piss off and leave us alone.'

The biker looked like he believed him then. 'If I go looking and it's not there I will come back for you. You understand me? You, your friends, and your brother.'

'Whatever fella.' Wilf held his hands up like he was done caring then turned back to the van leaving Florence feeling suddenly exposed.

'Come on,' Jasper said, tugging her arm.

'I mean it,' the biker yelled. 'If it's not there I will hunt you down.'

'I don't think you will,' Andrew said, stepping forward from the van.

Florence and Jasper looked at him in surprise and Wilf stopped and turned around.

Andrew was holding up his iPad. 'I recorded that whole conversation. It's already uploaded to my website but no one can see it yet. I've embargoed it till the end of the month. You leave us all alone and I'll delete it. If you don't, or anything happens to us, it'll go live. I've got nearly 19,000 followers. My last Vimeo went viral.' He glanced briefly at the men then cast his eyes to the ground.

The biker wearing the bandana stared at Andrew as if he were a dog that had just cocked its leg up against his bike.

The other guy nudged his arm. 'Come on. We're wasting time. They're just kids.'

After giving them another long, drawn out stare, he nodded, got back on his bike, and kicked the pedal. The roar of the machine made Andrew reach up to cover his ears.

149

The four of them watched as the bikers rode out of sight then Wilf turned to Andrew in disbelief. 'How the hell have you got nearly 19,000 followers for anything? You've only got three friends!'

Florence thought she saw Andrew smile to himself as he started back towards the van.

When they were pulling away Florence took out her notepad and added the word Vimeo to the list of words she didn't like. She stared at it for a moment then realised it was an anagram of movie. She warmed to it slightly more then and was considering crossing it out when Jasper nudged her knee under the table. 'What're you doing?'

'Nothing.' She put her notepad away again and was about to suggest another game of poker when the van began to shudder. It sounded like the engine was misfiring. Wilf revved it noisily and it jerked a few times before cutting out altogether. They rolled to a stop in the middle of the country road.

'Brilliant.' Wilf made a noise of frustration. He turned the key a few times, his head bent as though he was listening for something, then he got out, leaving the driver's door open, and lifted up the bonnet.

Jasper and Florence exchanged a look. 'Now what?' Jasper said.

They both got up and followed Wilf.

He was bent over the engine, inspecting it with a frown

of concentration. He stood up, wiped his hands on his T-shirt then walked to the back of the van. A moment later he returned with a toolbox. Jasper and Florence watched him take bits out, inspect them, then put them back again. 'I knew it. Water's got in the engine,' he said at last. He dropped a spanner back in the toolbox with a clatter then stared at the van, scratching his chin. 'It's not locked. It's the electrics. Maybe the solenoid. Best case scenario, it just needs to dry out. Some WD40 would help but there's none in the toolbox.' He raised his voice in the direction of the rear of the van. 'Andrew, is there a garage near here?'

Andrew came out with his iPad. He started tapping the screen. 'There's a petrol station about a mile and a half away if that's any good.' He pointed down a path that cut through a cornfield. There was a row of houses in the distance. 'Somewhere in that direction.'

Wilf thought for a minute. 'Right, I'll leave the bonnet up so it can start drying and I'm gonna walk to the shop. You want to come with me or stay here?'

'Stay here,' Andrew said.

'I wouldn't mind a walk actually,' Jasper said.

'But, what if those guys return?' Florence was watching the end of the road as though expecting them to appear at any moment.

Jasper frowned. 'Yeah, you're right. We should stick together.'

Andrew shook his head. 'They'll have found what they

came for soon enough. Coming back for us would be illogical. It only increases their risk of getting caught.'

'You think guys like that work on logic?' Wilf said. 'Jasper's right, let's stick together. We can push the van behind those trees so it's hidden from the road.'

Andrew looked as though he was going to argue then Wilf slapped him gently on the arm. 'Come on mate, the sooner it's sorted the sooner we can get to Howard.'

Andrew muttered to himself and reluctantly followed him.

Florence watched them wondering which was more surprising: Wilf's lack of put downs or Andrew being so quick to co-operate.

Florence and Jasper trailed behind. The heat was making Florence feel lazy and she tuned in to the sound of chirping crickets rather than bother to make small talk. The air smelt sweet and earthy and there was a shimmer in the distance which made her think of the holidays abroad she used to have with her family. They would camp every year in some remote part of France which was always a long, hot trek to a vast and empty beach. They didn't have holidays like that any more. They hadn't been anywhere for the last two years which was probably a good thing. Trapped on long car journeys and forced to entertain each other at night without separate rooms and a television to escape in front of, it'd be too obvious that they were all thinking about the things they could never acknowledge out loud. She shook the thoughts from her head.

Jasper shrugged his shirt off and tied it around his waist.

Florence felt her eyes drawn to him. She'd rarely seen him without a shirt. His T-shirt was baggy and his arms looked skinnier. He had a bruise just above his elbow, not purple like the one under his eye, but pale yellow and barely there.

He glanced at her and she looked away.

'Andrew's a dark horse, don't you think? Speaking up to those bikers like that.'

'I guess. He does tend to speak his mind though, doesn't he? It's why he ends up annoying Wilf all the time. I like it though. He's refreshingly honest.'

Jasper smiled to himself. 'You mean like when he asked Dennis's dad if there was any part of his body he hadn't tattooed?'

Florence laughed. 'That wasn't as bad as when he told Aggie she should save herself some time and serve tinned tomato soup because he likes it better and he preferred not to think about her having touched everything in his dinner.'

Jaspers eyes widened. 'Oh, that's brave. I'd rather take on those guys back there than insult Aggie's cooking.'

'She hasn't made soup since. Shame really, I thought it was nice.'

Jasper thought about it for a moment. 'You are right though. It's good not having to guess what he's thinking. Sometimes I think life would be easier if we could all read each other's minds.' He looked at Florence as though trying to read hers.

'I can think of super powers I'd rather have,' she said in

an attempt to change the subject. 'Like being invisible, or rewinding time like Superman.'

He nodded, amused, as though he knew what she was doing but figured he'd let her get away with it. 'I think the fact that Superman could fly was way more useful. How great would it be to fly? Better than going back in time. I mean, why go backwards? Surely what's done is done?'

She felt her throat constrict. Her change of subject was backfiring. 'I just think it'd be good to be able to fix your mistakes.'

'Ah, right. You mean like if you mess up an exam you could retake it without losing a year of your life? Or when you say something stupid in front of someone you really like, you could go back and say what you wanted to say: that witty thing you kick yourself for not saying in the first place.'

'Yeah, that sort of thing.' Florence answered without really having heard him. She was picturing a scene. One she'd replayed many times. Wishing she could go back in time and change it.

She was in the kitchen of a house she'd never been to before. It was hot and noisy and she was jostling for space with a room full of drunk, loud teenagers, most of them a year or two older than her. A sickly taste of cider was lingering in her mouth. It didn't seem to be having the same effect as it did on everyone else. She felt out of place. An alien in another world.

Rosie was looking at her with disappointment, her blue eyes pleading. 'But, we've not even been here an hour. Please don't go yet. Give it a chance.' Rosie wasn't a natural party-goer either. Even when they were little she'd always been the quieter one. She relied on Florence to make friends and break the ice. Florence had never minded, but lately her own confidence had faltered. She felt different, and not in a good way. She'd find herself worrying that everything she said was stupid. She'd started to avoid people at school, hiding in the library at lunchtime and turning down invites for trips to town and nights out. It had been a slow, creeping shift in her state of mind. She hadn't told Rosie because she hadn't wanted to admit it was taking hold. She was hoping it was a phase and she'd snap out of it soon enough. But it was getting worse not better. She was waking up with a feeling of dread, not wanting to get up in the morning, and now she was standing in the middle of a party, feeling panicked and trapped. Nausea was coming over her in waves.

She'd only agreed to come to the party because Rosie had heard that George was going to be there. A guy from her maths class she'd liked for ages. Rosie wanted Florence with her to give her the courage to talk to him but the vodka and Coke she was drinking was doing a better job of that than Florence could.

'Sorry, Rosie, I've got to go.'

'But . . . If you leave now I'll be on my own. Can't you just wait till we see somebody else I know?'

Florence was sweating, her heart pounding. What if she threw up, right now, in front of everyone? 'I'm really sorry, come back with me if you want but I've got to get out of here. I'm really not feeling so good.' She wished she were different – normal like everybody else.

Rosie looked hurt. 'Fine.' She reached for the bottle of vodka on the sideboard and topped herself up, drips of clear liquid spilling onto the floor. 'I'm going to see if there's anyone in the garden.' She was about to turn away then she stopped, adding, 'Are you walking back on your own? I don't think you should, you know.'

'It's okay, I'll call my mum.' Florence took out her phone and held it up to show her intent.

Rosie nodded. 'Right, well see you then.' She turned and started to pick her way through the dense room of people.

When Florence stepped out into the night she felt like she could breathe again. Her panic faded into a more familiar sense of sadness and frustration. She didn't want to call her mum and explain. Instead she put her phone back in her pocket and set off home.

That was the moment, Florence thought. The one she'd revisited every day for the past year. Every time she thought about it she wanted to cry with rage. She wanted to fly above the earth with her fists out in front of her. A superhero act of defiance. She wanted to turn back time and change everything. If she could, she'd go straight back to that party, and this time she'd stay.

'What are you thinking?' Jasper was searching her face, concerned.

'Oh, nothing.' She waved it away. She knew she couldn't keep dwelling on things she couldn't change. She could hear Howard telling her to learn from her mistakes. Move forward. Make everything that happens now count for something.

She made herself smile and Jasper instantly brightened.

'You're really pretty when you smile,' he said. 'You should smile all the time.'

She concentrated on the path ahead. 'Don't be silly.'

'You are.'

She couldn't say anything to that. She bit her lip to keep from smiling and kept walking, looking at the ground.

'You know, despite everything, this has actually been a really good day. Even if we can't find Howard, I'll still be glad I came. It's been good to spend some proper time with you.'

Florence wondered whether Jasper's 'you' included Andrew and Wilf. 'Me too.'

'In fact, I can't think of anything I'd rather be doing more than walking through a random field in Wales looking for a petrol station that sells WD40.'

'Oh, well, I don't know if I'd go that far.'

'It's true. This is the place to be. Right now.'

She shook her head. She never knew quite how seriously to take him. 'You're so upbeat, Jasper. I don't get how you ever ended up at Manor Lane.'

'Ninety per cent joyful, that's me. I'm going to get a T-shirt made.'

She wondered what that must be like. *Joyful* was one of those words that sounded like it made her feel, like *calm* and *ticklish*. 'What's the other ten per cent, then?'

He answered without even thinking. 'Terrified.' He held his fingers up to indicate it was small and insignificant. 'A tiny, ten per cent terrified, but I'm getting better at taming that part.' He slowed down and looked at her, searching her face like he was trying to figure something out. Part of her liked it, and part of her felt scared too. She felt herself starting to blush and wished she wasn't always so easy to read.

She made herself look away. 'I think I've spent the last year feeling numb. I can't imagine having those kinds of highs and lows. It must be exhausting.'

'Oh, it's not so bad. I've got this theory that I make more adrenaline than most people. It's like it's there all the time, just under the surface. I can live with it ninety per cent of the time. It's energising, you know? But there's a fine line between excitement and fear. It can change like the flick of a switch. One moment everything's awesome. The next you want to run away and hide.'

She wanted to take his hand in hers. Instead she supressed a smile. 'You sound like my neighbour's Labrador.'

He looked surprised that she was daring to tease him and his own smile grew. 'Yeah that's what it is, I'm a Labrador trapped in a teenager's body.'

'It'd explain why you're so friendly with everyone. And your twitchy energy. It's like you permanently need to get outside and run about in a field.'

'You may be onto something. Howard suggested I should take up running.'

'Maybe he should've thrown you a stick.'

His mouth dropped open and Florence laughed out loud.

Jasper elbowed her, making her veer off the path. 'Careful or I'll chase you.'

'Yeah? Then what? Will you bite my ankles?'

He exhaled comically, pretending he'd had enough, then hooked his arm around her neck, bringing his face close. 'I'd rather slobber in your ear.'

'No, don't!' She laughed louder and squealed as he buried his face in her neck, his breath warm and damp.

There was a sudden, loud whistle. 'Get a room, guys,' Wilf called out.

They stopped and looked up, momentarily disorientated.

Wilf and Andrew were waiting impatiently at the end of the field.

Florence and Jasper broke apart, laughing and breathless, and when they started walking again they were both grinning.

ULTIMATE QUESTIONS:
FAVOURITE HARRY POTTER SPELL?

FLORENCE: I'd like a time turner.

ANDREW: That's not a spell, it's a magical gadget. You can't have it.

FLORENCE: Okay then, *Expecto Patronum*. It's like what Howard's always saying about challenging dark thoughts. You can stop them if you believe what you're saying, it just takes a lot of practice. To do that, it's like real life magic.

JASPER: Yeah, it's just a pity you can't conjure up an adorable gambolling otter when you're doing it.

FLORENCE: That's why I follow @emergencyotters on Twitter.

JASPER: Ahh, good thinking.

FLORENCE: What about you?

JASPER: I dunno. Reading minds could be useful.

FLORENCE: *Legilimens*. But what if you saw something you didn't want to see?

JASPER: True. It's got to be *Lumos* then.

WILF: Don't be daft. Everyone's got a torch on their phone these days. What's that spell they use to fetch stuff?

JASPER AND FLORENCE: *Accio*.

WILF: See that one's actually useful. I'd use it all the time; *accio* spanner, *accio* tv remote, *accio* saucepan, *accio* ketchup . . .

ANDREW: *Silencio*.

Chapter Fifteen

The road on the other side of the field was a quiet back lane with a rough footpath that led past an assortment of old cottages. They followed it until they reached a petrol station. At the back of the forecourt was a small, single-storey flint building with a sign over the window marking it as a Post Office and General Store. An A-frame on the forecourt advertised that they also sold hot and cold drinks, top soil, tomato plants, bantam chickens and had a three-day service for dry cleaning. Another board offered car repairs, MOTs and tyres.

'This is great,' Jasper said. 'If you live in a place with not much passing trade you may as well be all the shops.'

Wilf opened the door of the shop and a bell chimed. There was a girl sitting behind the counter, her head bent over a book. She had dark, sleek hair cut in an angled bob and was wearing a tight grey vest top and a dog tag on a long chain. She looked older than them but not by much. When the bell sounded she looked up and closed her book without marking the page. 'Can I help you?'

'Yeah, is there someone here I can talk to about a problem with my van?' Wilf said.

'That'll be my dad. He's in the shed. Go out the way you came in, turn left and it's the big wooden building on the side.'

Wilf nodded and walked back out. Florence thanked her, ready to leave, but Andrew hesitated, looking at her book.

'*Fermat's Last Theorem*.'

'You've read it?'

'Of course.'

Her eyes lit up and she sat forward, staring at Andrew with a sudden intensity that made him hop from one foot to another and inspect the shelves behind her.

'You like it?'

'Well, yes, it's a compelling story, but it's quite simple.'

She snorted. 'Hey, he's bringing it to the people. What's wrong with making maths approachable? I love Simon Singh, he's amazing at that. He's a bit of a hero of mine, actually.'

Andrew looked put out, almost sulky. 'I think there are mathematicians more deserving of hero status. Archimedes, Pythagoras—'

'Yeah, yeah, and Newton and Turing, blah, blah, blah. You can have more than one hero you know.' She sat back and half smiled at him. 'Nice to meet a fellow maths geek. I'm usually the only one for miles.'

'Oh, well, I ...' Andrew made a noise like a nervous laugh and continued to be overly fascinated by the selection of canned produce behind her.

'I'm Megan. And you are ...?'

He blinked rapidly. 'Andrew. My friends and I, we're from Norwich. We've come looking for our therapist.'

Florence felt her cheeks instantly heat up.

Megan's eyebrows arched and she looked at Florence and Jasper as though checking this was true.

'You know how it is,' Jasper said with a self-deprecating grin.

She showed no sign of thinking that was anything other than normal. 'Sure, my therapist is a lifesaver. Literally. So, do you think he might be round here? Can I help? What's his name?'

'You might do, he's called Howard Green. His sister lives in Borth y Castell.' Andrew looked hopeful.

'Andrew, Wales isn't that small,' Jasper said. 'We're miles from—'

'Nice place,' Megan said, ignoring Jasper. 'The name doesn't ring a bell though.'

Andrew continued undeterred. 'His sister is Margot Green. She wrote the *Dragons of Bryn* stories.'

'Oh, right!' She pointed at them. 'Of course I know her, she's a legend round here. My little brother loves those books. Dressed up as Gruffydd for World Book Day and read a passage to the whole school. It was so cute I put it on YouTube.'

Florence was listening, mesmerised, to Megan's accent. She was transforming words, smoothing out their angles and edges and melting them into shapeless dips and curves.

'She's a recluse, isn't she? I swear I was reading something about her the other day.' Megan looked around as though there might be a book or an article to hand but drew a blank.

Jasper glanced at his watch then looked out of the window at Wilf. He was standing on the forecourt talking to a man with grey hair and a short, stocky build that matched Wilf's own. 'Don't worry, I'm sure we'll find them.'

'Well, good luck to you,' Megan said.

Jasper backed towards the door and Florence followed.

Andrew lingered at the counter as though he wanted to say something else and was struggling to find the words so they slipped out of the shop and left him to it.

Standing on the forecourt they looked back through the window, curious.

'Is it me or is Andrew attempting to chat her up?' Jasper said, as though he could hardly believe it.

'I dunno. There's definitely some kind of chemistry going on there,' Florence said.

Andrew looked like he had found his voice and was talking and gesticulating awkwardly as Megan listened with an amused but genuine smile.

Wilf joined them then. 'What's going on?' He peered through the window to see what Florence and Jasper were looking at. 'For goodness' sake, I thought it was me who was supposed to find it hard to stay focussed on a task.' He put his face close to the window then rapped on the glass with his knuckles.

Andrew jumped as though he'd been caught doing something wrong.

Wilf pointed impatiently at his watch.

'Ah, don't rush him,' Jasper said. 'How often do you think he meets a girl he really hits it off with?'

'He's already met a spaceman today. If he gets a girlfriend, he'll be unbearable.' He looked back at Andrew and tutted. 'Tell him he can catch us up. I'm gonna spray the engine and let it dry out some more before I try starting it again. With any luck we'll be back on the road in half an hour.' He tucked a can of WD40 into one of the side pockets of his shorts and started heading back towards the road.

Jasper and Florence sat under the shade of a tree, watching as Wilf tried to hammer out the dent in the side of the van where he'd clipped the signpost. As he hit the metal he muttered to himself in annoyance. 'God, I hate sheep. They're the most stupid bleeding animals ever created. They're worse than pigeons. They've got no sense of direction. They can't think for themselves. They can't even take a shit without getting it all over their backsides. Bloody clagnuts hanging off their arses.' He started talking in a slow, simple voice. 'Oh, I'll just stand here while something races towards me at speed with my stupid gob hanging open . . .'

Florence was laughing. 'Is that really a word? I swear my mum calls them dangle berries?'

Jasper shook his head. 'No, that's the bobbles you get on a jumper.'

'It's not funny.' Wilf whacked the inside of the door one last time then stood back to inspect the damage. Defeated, he rubbed his eyes and breathed slowly through his nose. 'This day is literally insane.'

'Actually sheep aren't as stupid as you think,' Andrew said. He was walking towards them, tapping on the screen of his iPad. 'They've got brains a bit like ours. They can recognise people and they form bonds with each other and have feelings.'

'Oh sure, it's uncanny. They'll be getting up on two legs and taking themselves to the library any day now.'

'Speaking of forming bonds,' Jasper said. 'What happened with you and that girl in the shop?'

Andrew looked momentarily confused, as though he'd forgotten already, then his face lit up. 'Oh, you mean Megan? She's so interesting. She's just finished her first year studying maths at Imperial in London. She never even went to school. She was home-educated. Spent most of her time helping out in the shop and reading books instead.'

'Impressive.' Florence imagined how good it would be to ditch school and read books all day, then remembered that would mean spending more time with her parents scrutinising her and thought better of it.

Andrew's iPad chimed. 'Megan says good luck getting the van started and her dad will come and help if you can't.'

'You're messaging her?'

'She's on WhatsApp.'

Wilf looked momentarily stunned. 'She gave you her contact details? You dog! I didn't think you had it in you.'

Andrew looked as though he didn't understand a word of what Wilf had just said.

Wilf leaned into the driver's side of the van and tried the engine. It burst loudly into life.

'Thank God for that!' Jasper jumped up then offered his hand to Florence.

Andrew followed them back to the van, his eyes still fixed on his iPad. 'Megan says "Whoop!"' he said, climbing back inside.

The closer they got to Borth y Castell the more Florence's thoughts turned to Howard and why they'd come. She chewed on her lip, staring at the mountainous landscape cutting through the sky ahead. It was so far removed from the scenery back home that she struggled to place Howard in it. She'd never seen him outside Manor Lane. She knew him only as the man in comfy jumpers who strode the corridors of Manor Lane with a coffee in one hand and someone's paperwork in another, or who sat in his office with his back to the window, listening to her as if he were tuned in to an interesting play on the radio.

Howard knew more about her than anyone else she knew. He knew what she did at the weekend and what her family and friends were like. She'd described enough of her house and garden, her cat and her street, that he could no doubt picture them well. He knew about her childhood and her teenage years and everything that led up to that night a year ago. There was nothing left out.

She realised now that as much as she thought she knew him, it was only snippets of the whole person. When he talked about his life he never gave much away. She knew more about his likes and dislikes than his personal life or family. She knew that he didn't enjoy learning until he went to university, that he'd been inspired to change the course of his career after a bout of depression. She knew a lot about which films and books he enjoyed, that he was interested in politics and history and didn't like watching sport. She knew his thoughts on guilt and depression, happiness and anger, and his strong belief in a person's ability to change. She knew that he preferred to listen to current affairs and talk shows on the radio and had never really understood or enjoyed music. She knew he liked cats but didn't know if he owned one. She didn't know if he was married or divorced or lived alone. She wondered if he still got depressed sometimes. If it was stressful working at Manor Lane, hearing about other people's problems all day. Surely that kind of job would take its toll on anybody. Moods were catching, weren't they?

She pictured Howard now, in a small Welsh cottage that

like him was friendly and old-fashioned and a little dishevelled around the edges. He'd be sitting in an armchair with a view of the garden and a well-stocked bookcase beside it. She hoped he wouldn't mind them turning up, that he'd hear them out and appreciate the gesture. She wanted him to come back to Manor Lane, not just for their sakes, but for the ones who came next.

Thinking about all the advice he'd given her, and the strategies he'd taught her for the times she wasn't coping, she said to no one in particular, 'What's the best advice Howard's given you?'

'Advice isn't the reason I like seeing Howard,' Andrew said. 'I like him because he's intelligent and he listens to me and he doesn't do the kind of annoying stuff people usually do when I'm talking to them, like laugh, or walk off, or tell me I'm doing something wrong.'

'Surely he's given you advice though, Andrew?' Jasper said. 'He's always got something useful to say.'

Andrew considered it for a moment. 'I suppose he did suggest that I ask more questions. I told him that I find it difficult to make friends with people my age and he said it helps if you ask them things. The kind of things I'd really like to know the answer to so I'd listen, because people like to be listened to, and because Howard says you learn more when you're not talking.'

Florence smiled. She could just imagine Howard saying that. It was the reason he knew more about her than the other way round.

'The trouble is, I can't usually think of anything to ask, because most people aren't very interesting. Then when I met Megan I thought about what Howard said so I asked her how she knew so much about maths. She told me about her degree and she was very interesting, so I asked if I could have her phone number and she gave it to me, so I guess asking questions turns out to be really good advice.'

Wilf snorted. 'First time lucky there, mate. I can tell you from experience, nine times out of ten you'll get burned.'

'Maybe different advice works for different people,' Florence said, unable to keep the note of sarcasm out of her voice. Asking for a phone number on the basis of something more meaningful than how hot a girl was might have been better advice for Wilf.

'I'll say this for Howard. He's one of those guys who knows something about everything. You know the best advice Howard ever gave me?' Wilf said. 'To try reverse searing a steak.'

Jasper laughed. 'Wow. I'll bet he's thrilled his years studying psychology haven't been wasted on you.'

'I'm serious. He's changed my life with that tip. There's a science to it. A hot sear does something to the molecules in the meat that gives the meat a crust that's so delicious, it's like a savoury flavour bomb, I'm telling you.'

'It's called the Maillard reaction,' Andrew said. 'It's a chemical reaction between the amino acids and sugars at high heat which boosts the presence of umami.'

Wilf nodded. 'Yeah, that's pretty much what Howard said, only he made it sound interesting.'

Florence repeated the word in her head, liking the way it sounded. 'How do you spell it?'

'U-M-A-M-I,' Andrew said. 'The Japanese call it the fifth sense: sweet, salt, bitter, sour, umami. I guess we'd call it savoury. You get it in Parmesan and Marmite and really good gravy.'

'That's a really great word,' Florence said.

'Yep. Best advice he gave me for sure,' Wilf said. 'I Googled it and found a recipe online and it was like . . . ' He made a gesture to show his head exploding.

'Deep.' Jasper nodded with mock gravity.

'What about you then, Jasper?' Florence said. 'What's been Howard's best advice?'

'Hmm, I guess the one that sticks out most in my mind today would be that there's always something in your future you'll be glad you stuck around for. He's definitely right about that.' He caught Florence's eye and smiled as though they shared a secret. She felt her stomach flip.

'That's not advice,' Andrew said. 'It's an observation.'

'Right, thanks, Andrew.' Jasper expression turned to amusement.

'Well, it's a good observation,' Florence said.

'Yeah,' Wilf added. 'Hang in there, because tomorrow you might have the best steak of your life.'

'Or meet an astronaut, and make a new friend,' Andrew said.

172

'Or drive across the country with three awesome people in a van with a freaking union jack on it.' Jasper gestured dramatically to the front of the van.

'Hell yes!' Wilf cheered.

Andrew's iPad pinged again. 'Today's been the best day of my life,' he said.

Chapter Sixteen

It was nearly seven in the evening by the time they finally arrived at Borth y Castell. A sign announced their arrival as they drove down a steep, narrow road lined with dense trees. They passed a golf course and a handful of houses and it seemed like a small and ordinary place until a view of the coast opened up ahead of them.

'Oh, it's so pretty!' Florence leant against the back of the seat, taking in the scene.

Neat white houses hugged the hills which surrounded a narrow harbour, where fishing boats and small yachts bobbed on sparkling water. On the far side of the inlet, where the coastline jutted out to sea, the remains of a small, turreted castle stood on a rocky mound.

'Andrew, come and see.'

'I know what it looks like; I'm looking at it on Google Maps. If you follow the road down to the High Street there's a car park on the sea front.'

They passed a row of shops, a post office, a café and a travel agency, all of them shut. At the front of the harbour there was a small car park, only a few spaces remaining despite the closed shops. Wilf swung the van into a spot by the sea wall that had an uninterrupted view of the coastline and castle. They got out quickly, desperate to stretch their legs and get a proper look at the view. The cry of seagulls circling the boats and the smell of fish and seawater immediately made Florence think of her childhood holidays, before her parents decided French campsites had more appeal. They used to go with Rosie and her parents; they'd been family friends since she and Rosie were born. Her head filled with a hundred little snapshots of hours spent playing on the beach, building piles of sand to jump in and collecting shells. She felt a shiver of familiarity.

Jasper inhaled deeply and took in the view, then he turned and surveyed the village behind them. The houses on the hill were flanked by dense green woodland. Beyond that was a mountain range. Pale grey peaks stood out against the blue sky on the horizon. He pointed out the highest peak. 'I think that might be Snowdon, you know.'

Florence thought she might have been there on a holiday once when she was very small. She had a vague memory of a photo of her travelling up a mountain on a train, looking down at the clouds beneath them. There were no clouds around it today. She imagined there must be people there right now, looking down at the coastline where they were stood, admiring the view of the sea. 'This place is stunning.'

'Yep. If I lived here I don't think I'd ever want to leave,' Jasper said. His attention switched back to the many houses on the hill. 'I don't know how we're going to find Howard here though.'

The task ahead of them dawned on Florence and she realised they had underestimated how difficult it might be. She'd imagined a tiny village, a place where everyone knew everybody else's business. That might have been the case in the winter, when the holiday homes sat empty and only the locals remained. Right then it had the atmosphere of a tourist spot, with people sitting on the sea wall, packing up after a day on the beach, or slowly browsing the windows of closed shops and busy restaurants. None of them would know anything about the people who lived there. Where would they start?

'Well, I don't know about you but I reckon we're going to need to find somewhere to sleep overnight, probably somewhere we can pitch a tent next to the van, and I'm gonna need some food,' Wilf said.

Andrew was wringing his hands, also studying the houses on the hillside. 'But, we need to find Howard.'

'I doubt Howard's gonna offer us all a bed for the night whether we find him or not so I think it's more important we sort somewhere to crash before it gets dark. Howard can always wait till the morning. We'll have more luck when the shops are open and we can ask the locals.'

'No!' Andrew looked horrified at the idea of waiting any longer. He stared again at the houses as though willing Howard to appear and solve the problem.

Wilf sighed. 'Okay. How about I go look for some food and somewhere to pitch and you guys can start asking people about Margot in the places that are still open.'

Jasper nodded. 'Good plan.'

Satisfied, Andrew set off at a pace towards the High Street.

Jasper and Florence hurried after him.

'Ring me if you find out anything, but don't take ages, yeah?' Wilf called after them. 'I'm bloody starving.'

They were getting nowhere fast. People either shrugged, clueless, or looked at them with suspicion. The few people who admitted knowing who Margot was were quick to point out that she was the kind of person who kept herself to herself and didn't have much to do with the village. The owner of an Indian takeaway was a little friendlier, suggesting they try Merfyn, the manager of the post office who apparently knew everyone.

'But, it's Sunday tomorrow,' Florence said. 'Won't it be shut?'

'It's a paper shop too. He'll be there from eight o'clock, has been every day since I can remember. He'll know who you're looking for.'

They thanked him and left the restaurant then wandered back to the post office, which they'd passed earlier and dismissed for being shut. They stared at it as though it might hold a clue. There was a blind pulled down, obscuring the window. A list of opening times on the door confirmed it was open on Sunday at 8 a.m. and several flyers on the window advertised everything from a table-top sale in a church to a quiz night at the Ship Inn that evening.

'We could try asking in the pub,' Andrew said. 'Landlords know everyone too, don't they?'

'The ones who drink, maybe,' Jasper said. 'It doesn't sound like Margot socialises much.'

'Howard might though,' Florence said.

Andrew perked up. 'Yes, if he often visits his sister he might know some local people to meet up with, or he might just like to sit at a bar and people watch.'

A shrill whistle behind them made them look around. Wilf was walking towards them across the car park. The van was no longer there. He pointed impatiently at his watch. 'Come on guys, let's eat.'

'Okay, Andrew, I like your thinking,' Jasper said, 'but let's make sure Wilf's fed before we let him loose in a pub.'

Wilf led them down a wooded coastal path that opened out onto a small, secluded beach with a car park behind. The van was reversed up to the edge of the sand and Wilf had already pitched the tent nearby, facing the water. Gentle waves lapped between two rocky outcrops which framed the view of the castle on the other side of the inlet. There was no one else around.

'Wow, this is so pretty.' Florence got her phone out and took a photo of the view.

Wilf unlocked the back of the van and took a large frying pan out of the cupboard. 'I got food. Not much choice on our budget so I got bacon and eggs, beans, bread, tomatoes. Enough for breakfast too. There's already oil and ketchup, salt and pepper in the van.' He picked up a spatula and pointed it at them. 'Who's hungry?'

Jasper looked non-committal and Andrew eyed Wilf's kitchen set up with suspicion.

'I also brought some water back for drinking, cooking, brushing your teeth, whatever.' He gestured at a large white container with a tap on the bottom.

Andrew's eyes widened. 'I'm not drinking out of that.'

'Your choice.' Wilf flicked a tea towel over his shoulder and lit the burners.

'Do you need any help?' Florence offered.

'I'm good, ta.' Wilf set to work and Florence stayed and watched. She could tell he cooked a lot. He did it without even pausing to think. Florence would have been timing everything, getting stressed or distracted, but Wilf looked like he could cook with his eyes closed. His mood had vastly improved and he was more relaxed than he'd been all day. He was enjoying himself.

There were only two burners and not much space so he cooked the bacon first, wrapping it in foil to keep it warm then cracked the eggs into the pan with one hand, frying

179

bread in the gaps. He flipped them just at the moment when they were perfectly crisp and golden. The smell was making Florence's mouth water.

Andrew appeared behind her. He eyed the food curiously, hungry but impatient to get going. 'After we've eaten we were saying we should go to the pub,' he said.

Wilf looked stunned for a moment then laughed. 'For a minute there, Andrew, I thought you suggested going to the pub.'

'I did. We should. I was thinking we might see Howard, or maybe the landlord knows him or his sister. It's got to be worth asking. We walked all the way up and down the village and I only saw one pub. The Ship Inn. It's just at the bottom of the High Street, over the road there.' He pointed to the row of trees behind the van which screened the car park from the road.

'I guess it's worth a try. Are you buying a round?'

'I wasn't suggesting we go for a drink, Wilf. I don't have any money, you know it got stolen, and I'm only sixteen and . . .'

'Yeah, yeah, Andrew, I know. Fortunately I came prepared.' He opened the cupboard above his head and took out a bottle of vodka and four stacked plastic cups.

'Oh, I don't know if I . . . I never . . . ' Andrew pulled at the neck of his T-shirt and blinked rapidly.

'Well, I don't know about you but after the day I've had I'm gonna be having a drink.' He passed Jasper the bottle and cups. 'Set 'em up.'

Jasper looked at Florence. 'You want one?'

Florence hardly ever drunk. She'd been wary of it for a long time. She was scared of how it made her feel: exaggerated and out of control. Her feelings weren't usually the kind of feelings you wanted to exaggerate. Maybe today is different though, she thought. She felt good. She was enjoying the moment. 'Yeah, maybe just a bit.'

The sky glowed with golden light as the sun set beyond the sea. Its reflection burned a glistening path in the water leading all the way back to the beach where they sat. It was as though they were the only people on the planet and the display was just for them. Florence couldn't remember the last time she'd stopped and watched the sun set.

'Is it always this beautiful?' she said to no one in particular.

'Not where I live.' Wilf took another swig of vodka. 'I sometimes watch it set behind the back of the social club opposite my house. The windows glow like the place is on fire. I have to stop and look because once it actually was on fire and two people died: the druggie who started it and a tramp sleeping on the back stairs.'

'Oh my God, that's awful.' Florence heard Jasper snort and nudged him. 'Don't laugh!'

'I'm not laughing. Not really. It's just that sometimes it's so bad you have to.'

'It's true,' Wilf said. 'Sometimes you don't see how bad your life is till you step away and look at it from a distance.

All day I've been thinking how good it is to get away from there. I just wish I didn't have to go back.'

'You have to go back,' Andrew said. 'How else will we get home? I have to be home on Monday. Mondays are my favourite days.'

Florence wasn't looking forward to Monday. Her parents would likely be overly scrutinising her, worried in case the anniversary had triggered something dark and worrying. She thought about Jasper going home to an empty house and felt part envious and part sad. He had the freedom of no one there, breathing down his neck – but then Jasper wasn't the kind of person who enjoyed being alone.

'When's your mum back from Spain, Jasper?'

He snorted again, drained his cup then looked down at the sand and sighed. 'Look, you may as well know. My mum's not actually in Spain.'

'What?'

All three of them looked at him.

'She's actually working at a tapas bar on the High Street. She's going out with the owner so she sleeps at his most nights. She's not been taking her medication. She's bi-polar and right now she's having a manic episode. She thinks she's in love and her new bloke's some kind of genius business man who's going to give her a better life. What's really happening is he's giving her some bollocks story about investing in a bar when he's actually just stealing her money and using it to pay off his debts. I looked him up online. He's been bankrupt three times. I tried to tell her this morning. She didn't take it well.'

Florence's jaw dropped as it dawned on her what that meant. 'It was ... You mean ... She did that?' She looked at his cheek which, like the clouds on the horizon, had now turned a deep shade of purple.

'Yeah. I locked her out after she got verbal with me and she bashed the door in. It's great back home, hey?' He swallowed hard and glanced up. His eyes were glistening.

Florence felt sick. 'Oh God, I'm really sorry, Jasper.'

Wilf leaned over to top up Jasper's cup with a generous slug of vodka. 'What a bitch.'

He shook his head. 'No. She's not. Don't say that. She doesn't know what she's doing. She just needs to start taking her meds again. I need Howard to talk to her. She listens to him.'

Florence understood now why Jasper was so keen to come. 'We'll find Howard. It'll be okay.' Florence wished she could say more. Do more. Her words sounded empty.

Wilf shook his head. 'You two. You need to stop seeing Howard as the solution. He's a bloke not a magician. The best thing you can do is get out of there. Don't let other people's problems drag you down. I should know that better than anyone, right?'

'Yeah, so you should know it's not that easy. I can't leave her. I'm all she's got, and she's all I've got.'

'Well, you've got us now. We've all been through it. We've

got your back, right?' Wilf looked at Andrew and Florence to agree with him.

'You have,' Andrew said. 'We're your friends.'

Florence wanted to add her own voice to theirs but didn't trust herself to speak. She reached out and squeezed his hand instead, something she'd been longing to do all day. When she moved to take her hand back, Jasper held on to it, his fingers closing on hers. 'Thanks guys.'

Andrew looked around impatiently at the darkening trees behind him. 'I really do think we should go to the pub now.'

Wilf laughed. 'How can you be so right yet so wrong at the same time, Andrew?'

'I don't understand what you mean.'

Wilf drained his vodka and stood up, brushing the sand off his legs. 'You're just itching to go to the pub because you think we'll find Howard, but the sad truth is we're on a hiding to nothing with only enough funds for a couple of beers between the four of us. Even if we did find Howard there's not much he can do to help us now and I doubt very much us turning up on his doorstep would be any help to him. You're right though, Andrew, we should go to the pub, but we should go like normal people do. Have a drink and a laugh and forget all this mess. Don't you want to know what it feels like?'

Andrew looked glum. 'I don't really like drinking.'

Florence could feel the vodka she'd had starting to take effect, making her feel woozy and disconnected. She looked into her cup. It was empty. 'I'm not sure I should have any more.'

'Fine,' Wilf said. 'Two beers, two tap waters, let's just go and at least pretend we're normal.' He started putting things back in the van and Andrew went to fetch his iPad.

'Jasper, are you okay?' Florence said, when they were out of earshot.

He nodded and smiled at her. One of those sad smiles. 'I don't know why I didn't tell you earlier. It doesn't make any difference really.'

'It's okay. You don't have to tell me anything you don't want to.'

'I know, but I do want to. That's the thing. I feel like I could tell you anything.'

Her stomach swooped as though she'd just missed a step on the stairs. How could Jasper ever really like her? He didn't know her. Not the worst of her. She wanted to be able to tell him everything but the thought made her heart race and her mouth dry up. I don't deserve to be happy, she thought, feeling as though the gloomy darkness behind her was creeping closer.

'Are *you* okay?' Jasper said, looking suddenly worried.

She didn't want Jasper to worry. She didn't want to ruin the day by letting the negative thoughts in. Ants, Howard called them. Automatic negative thoughts. They scurried around inside your head, swarming until they were an army that could overpower you. You had to crush every one,

185

Howard had told her. You had to hit them with a powerful positive thought until eventually you trained your brain into thinking positive.

'I'm good,' she said, standing up. 'I. Am. Good.' She staggered a little, unsteady on the sand. 'Woah, that vodka was strong.'

'Come on. I've got you.' Jasper put an arm around her shoulders and steered her off the beach.

Florence's notebook

A.N.T.S

Unhelpful negative thought	Positively crushingly good thought
I don't deserve to feel good	I deserve to feel wonderful and enjoy life and laugh loud and proud!
I'm a bad friend	I am a loyal and caring friend. I am not perfect but I will do what I can, when I can, to be there for anyone who asks.

Unhelpful negative thought	Positively crushingly good thought
It's my fault	I am not responsible for the actions of others. I don't always do the right thing but everyone makes mistakes. I have to forgive myself, learn and move on.
Everyone hates me	Not everyone will like me but there are plenty of people who love me and care about me and I know I am loveable and likeable person.
I'm a terrible person	I am a good person. I'm not a perfect person, but I am a good person and sometimes I am awesome!
What's the point?	The point is not clear until you do it. Do it and you'll be so glad you did. That is the point!

Unhelpful negative thought	Positively crushingly good thought
I can't do it	~~Oh shut up!~~ I can do anything. I am a warrior!

Chapter Seventeen

The pub fell momentarily silent when they walked in.

Florence felt like all eyes were on them. She was conspic-
uous. A stranger. She held her head up and told herself that
she was normal. *Nothing to see here.* She walked as confidently
as she could to a table in a nook in the corner of the room,
Jasper close behind. Andrew and Wilf headed for the bar.
Andrew looked taller and older than any of them, despite
being the youngest, and Wilf had a fake ID. They'd have
better luck going to the bar alone, they'd agreed outside.

The regulars quickly lost interest and went back to their
business and the hum of background noise returned. A short,
balding man stood in the middle of the room and began to
read out the rules of the pub quiz.

Florence and Jasper settled opposite each other in a stall
with high backs, conveniently shielding them from view.

The window beside them was misted over. Jasper wiped
his hand across it and together they peered out at the view of

the sea across the road. It was now too dark to see more than the lights from the houses on the steep hill across the water and the scattered reflections of light on the boats moored in the harbour. 'Maybe we should all stay here,' Jasper said. 'Live out of the van for a while. Get some part-time work. Never go back. Do you think Wilf would mind?'

'Probably not, but Andrew would freak.' Florence thought about home and absently reached for the bracelet Kimi had given her, stroking the smooth cat charm that dangled from it. The thought of staying was a nice dream but she knew she couldn't really consider it. She'd only give her parents more to worry about, and Kimi had been a good friend. She was worth going back for.

'What're you thinking?'

'Oh, just about home, you know, like maybe going back's not so bad after all. I think I've had enough of Manor Lane now. I feel like I need to move on, catch up with my A levels. I might have to retake a year but it's not long and then maybe I can go to uni. Escape properly. Like normal people do.' She smiled ironically.

'I guess.' Jasper looked momentarily sad. 'I'm going to miss Manor Lane though. I suppose I already do. It's not the same without Howard and it won't be the same without you guys.' He smiled as he picked at the edges of a beer mat. 'What am I going to do without Andrew's gadget guidance? And how will I get by without Wilf telling me to fatten up and questioning my sexuality? And who will help me answer the important questions in life like *most powerful wizard*?' He batted her hand with the mat and gave her a significant nod. 'And who'll be there to talk to me when I want a friend who really gets me?'

Florence gave him a sceptical look. 'I bet you've got loads of friends back in college.'

'Not like you.'

'Weird, you mean?'

'No. Not weird. Not at all. You're different, in a good way. You're interesting, and caring, and easy to talk to.'

She looked down at the table. *I wish that was true*, she wanted to say. *You don't know everything.*

'You're also really pretty.' He was resting his chin on his hand and gazing at her. She wondered whether that was the vodka talking.

'Stop.' She was blushing now. Too aware of his eyes on her.

'It's true. You're very naturally pretty – kind of pale and pointy, like a woodland creature.'

She couldn't help but laugh at that. He'd managed to pick out the two things she liked least about her face. 'I'm not sure that's complimentary.' She looked out of the window again, searching for something she could change the subject with.

'I'm terrible at talking to girls, aren't I?'

'Jasper, you're good at talking to everyone. It's why it's hard to take you seriously sometimes. You just . . . I dunno, you're charming. A charmer, maybe.'

He looked hurt. 'You think I'm not genuine?'

'No, you're definitely genuine. Genuinely nice. But you're nice to everyone, you know?'

'I suppose I am a people pleaser.'

'You're a crowd pleaser.'

He laughed and picked up a beer mat, turning it in his fingers. His feet were tapping a rhythm, his legs moving up and down. That nervous energy. 'There are, absolutely, some people I like more than others. Some people. One person,' he corrected, pointing the beer mat at her. 'Who, more than anyone else I've ever met, I want to like me.'

She bit her lip and waited. He was going to have to say it. She could never just assume he was talking about her.

Andrew and Wilf appeared between them and Florence finally took a breath.

Jasper smiled and gave her a look that said *you'll keep* then turned to the others. 'How'd you get on?'

Andrew looked glum but Wilf said, 'Good. Beer's cheap round here.' He had a bag of crisps dangling from between his teeth and was holding a pint of beer and three half pints of Coke. He dished them out on the table.

Andrew slumped onto the bench seat next to Florence. 'None of them know Howard. They've all heard of his sister but they're all saying the same: that she doesn't socialise, she's a recluse, and likes to keep herself to herself.'

'Well, I guess coming here was always going to be a long shot,' Jasper said.

Andrew looked unsatisfied. 'I don't believe the landlord

193

though. I think he knows where she lives but he doesn't want to tell us. He thinks I'm some kind of weirdo.'

Wilf sat opposite him. 'You are a weirdo. He was being friendly till you butted in and said "just tell us where she lives" like some kind of crazy stalker.'

Andrew sighed. 'Why can't people just say what they're thinking instead of having to work up to it all the time?'

'I'll tell you what I'm thinking,' Wilf said. 'I'm thinking we came all this way for nothing but a load of grief and a shitload more when I get home.'

'I suppose it was a pretty crazy plan,' Florence said.

'I told you, it's not a plan, it's an objective, and it's not over yet,' Andrew said. 'We've not done what we came here to do.'

Wilf pointed at him. 'You. Are a dog with a bone.'

'I don't see what more we can do,' Florence said.

'There's still that guy at the post office. We can ask him in the morning.'

'Maybe send Florence for that job, Andrew,' Wilf said. 'I don't think you're our lucky charm. And prepare yourself for disappointment. We're heading back at lunchtime whether we like it or not.'

They all sat in silence for a moment, momentarily lost in their own thoughts, then a microphone squeaked and a man announced in a thick Welsh accent, 'Okay everyone, pens at the ready, here's your first question.'

Andrew took a sheet of paper and a pencil out of his pocket.

Jasper looked baffled. 'What? So we're doing the quiz now?'

'I love quizzes.'

'I couldn't stop him,' Wilf said.

'There might be some sport questions or films or books. You might be able to help.'

'Yeah, thanks, Andrew. You'd better win is all I can say. That cost me my last four quid. I could've got another pint out of that.'

'The winning team gets the kitty and a round of drinks,' Andrew explained to Jasper and Florence like it was a no-brainer, then held up a hand as he listened to the quizmaster.

'Which club does Rafa Benítez currently manage?'

Andrew tapped the table with his pencil. 'Can't he be more specific? What sort of club?' He attempted to stand up but Wilf tugged him back down.

'It's Newcastle, you muppet.'

'But, that's a city?'

'Football club, he means football. Jeez.' He smacked a hand on his face.

'In *Strictly Come Dancing* . . .' the quizmaster started.

Andrew groaned and put his head in his hands. 'What kind of quiz is this?'

Jasper smiled and sat up. 'Don't panic folks, I've got this.'

The street was empty when they left the pub, their laughter suddenly amplified in the still night air.

Wilf raised his bottle of vodka to the crescent moon and howled. 'What a team.'

'I still don't see why we had to spend all the winnings on alcohol.' Andrew stiffened as Wilf slapped him on the back.

'I bought you a bag of crisps, didn't I?'

'And I still don't think it was much of a quiz. How does it test your intelligence to know who the judges of *The Voice* are?'

'Who cares? We won! You've been moaning all night. You're lucky the landlord didn't bar us after you told him what you thought of his quiz.'

'He clearly doesn't care who he serves. He didn't even ask for your ID and it's well past closing time.'

'Alright, grandma. Free booze and a late-night lock-in and still you moan. You don't have to sleep in my van tonight, you know.' They crossed the street.

Florence hung behind and looked at her watch.

It was five to midnight. Her stomach turned over and her good mood evaporated. In just a few minutes it would be the anniversary of that day. She realised then why she'd come all this way. She'd known it all along, really. Howard was just an excuse. She'd been trying to escape, and now she knew she couldn't. The day would come no matter where she was.

She could hear Wilf laughing and felt a guilty unease for having spent the night enjoying herself in a pub, miles away from home. It felt wrong now. Disrespectful.

Jasper dropped back from the other two and appeared next to her. 'Are you okay?'

'Yeah. Maybe too much to drink.'

'There's some water back in the van.'

A sudden flood of emotion washed over her, catching her off guard. 'I'll catch you up.'

'Don't be silly, I'm not leaving you in the street by yourself.'

She remembered the last time she was in a street in the dark by herself, walking away from that party, glad to be alone, glad to be leaving all those people behind, people she had nothing in common with, except Rosie. Her stomach clenched. She put a hand to her mouth then hurried across the road, leaning over the sea wall just in time to be sick.

The night was warm and muggy but she trembled anyway. She was sitting cross-legged on the sand, watching as the sea lapped rhythmically in front of her. She'd brushed her teeth with Andrew's toothpaste and some bottled water, swilling her mouth out behind a rock, but the taste of alcohol still lingered. She heard footsteps approach in the sand then felt the weight of a blanket around her shoulders. Jasper sat beside her, put an arm around her, and pulled her to him. It felt so nice she started to cry.

'I'm sorry,' she said, wiping her nose with the back of her hand, no longer caring that she was a mess. 'I was fine. I thought I'd be fine. I thought I could keep busy and it wouldn't bother me and it was working, but now it's Sunday and it all feels different, and I just feel so bad because I was enjoying myself, and it was like it never happened. I haven't felt like that in ages. Not all year. Not really.'

'You're not making much sense, Florence.' Jasper pushed her hair away from her face so he could see her better. 'You want to talk about it? You don't have to, but I'm here if it helps.'

She didn't want to talk about it. She was too scared. If a bad person did a good thing they were still a bad person. If a good person did a bad thing they became a bad person. It didn't matter what she was before or what she'd become, she'd always be defined by this one bad thing. She'd said that to Howard once. He'd had an answer for her but she couldn't remember it now. Negative thoughts were crowding her head. She realised it was pointless fighting them. She had to tell him. If she didn't she'd be living a lie. 'You'll hate me.'

He shook his head. 'Not possible.'

'I'm a bad person.'

'Never.'

Her chest was tight. A familiar ache that wasn't going away. Tears fell from her chin. 'A year ago today. My best friend, Rosie. She died, and it was my fault.'

There was a silence. 'What do you mean? Don't be silly.'

'It's true.'

He shifted so he was sitting in front of her. 'Florence, I'm sure it can't be true.'

'It is. I let her down. I was a terrible friend.' She felt like she was on a ledge, about to fall. She took a deep breath.

'I grew up with Rosie. My parents were friends with her parents. Our mums were pregnant at the same time. Rosie was born three days later than me. We used to pretend we were sisters. I was the older one, always looking out for her. Rosie was my best friend. We used to hang out at the weekend and holidays. We did everything together. We went to different schools until year seven, when we moved up to high school. I was so excited. I'd never had any close friends at school. I never really felt like I fitted in. I thought that having Rosie with me would make everything better.' She rubbed her eyes with the back of her hands then opened them, blinking. She wasn't crying any more. Rosie was alive in her mind.

'It didn't quite work out like that though. Rosie was shy but people naturally liked her. She was prettier and funnier than me. She made new friends from the start. She included me too. She always did. Kimi was nice and became my friend, but the others – girls like Jess – they weren't like me. They were loud and popular and always going out with someone. Rosie got on with everyone but she still kind of clung to me. She was still like a little sister, needing attention and approval all the time.

'Around the start of year eleven I started to feel different. Worse, somehow. I can't really explain it. I'd just wake up with this feeling of dread. I'd spend the weekends in bed. I

199

didn't want to take a shower or go out or do anything. I just wanted to hide from everyone. I thought I was weird and different and rubbish at everything. I could tell Rosie's friends didn't want to hang out with me. A couple of them started messaging me on Facebook, calling me names, telling me I wasn't welcome in their group. I closed my account and they started texting me instead. *Rosie only hangs out with you because she feels sorry for you,* or, *Why don't you just kill yourself?* It was horrible. I stopped going out at the weekends and made excuses when Rosie wanted to do stuff. She used to worry that it was something she'd done. She'd take it personally and get upset and ask what she'd done wrong. The others couldn't understand why she kept bothering with me.

'Last year, after GCSEs, there was this party. A girl from sixth form invited Jess and she asked if we could all go. We were meant to go to her house first but Rosie couldn't get there till later. She had some family thing so she asked if she could go with me later on. I said yes, even though I didn't want to go. I was trying to convince myself I could still join in and enjoy myself like everyone else was doing. I wanted to feel normal. Rosie got dropped off at mine and we walked there. Her mum was going to pick us up at midnight. When we arrived we couldn't see the others. We hung out in the kitchen and drank cider. Rosie kept downing them but I didn't like the way it made me feel. I felt awkward. I wished I hadn't gone. Eventually I told Rosie I was going home. I knew I was letting her down. She had no one else to hang out with but I couldn't stay. She pleaded with me not to leave her. She said she'd be on her own but I went anyway.' Florence's voice was shaking and she paused for a minute. She wished she could leave it there but she'd gone this far. She had to get it all out now.

'I walked home and when I got back I got straight into bed. I had my phone with me and Rosie kept texting. I sent a few back but mostly I just read them and didn't reply. I could tell she was drunk. At first she sounded like she was having a good time. She'd been drinking and dancing with the others. Then this guy she liked, George, turned up with a girl. She was really upset. She'd built herself up to tell him she liked him and all of a sudden there was no point. She said she wanted to go home then and the texts stopped for a while. I fell asleep but then my phone woke me up buzzing. There were a whole bunch of new messages. All this stuff about how she just wanted to be liked. How she wished she could be more like me because I didn't care what other people thought. She said that Jess and the others had never liked her. They were freezing her out and she didn't blame them. She hated herself. She felt unlovable.' Florence's voice cracked. 'I was going to reply. I should have replied straight away. I should have told her how great she was and how much I loved having her as my friend. I was mad at her for caring what Jess thought when she and her friends had been so awful to me.'

Jasper reached out for her hand but she pulled it away.

'No, don't be nice to me. I don't deserve it. There's more. She said she wanted to die. She said she couldn't keep trying any more. I didn't know how to reply to that. I thought she was being drunk and dramatic. She could be so over-the-top and emotional, always asking for reassurance. I didn't take it seriously. I thought I was the one who was struggling. She was coping. This was just a blip. She'd be okay.' Tears clouded her vision. 'I ignored her. I figured it'd be easier to speak to her in the morning when she'd sobered up and was calmer and I could speak to her properly. I turned my phone off and fell asleep.'

She closed her eyes and Rosie was gone.

'My mum's voice woke me up. She was calling for my dad. I heard him run across the landing and down the stairs. He started talking on the phone. My mum was crying. This awful high pitch cry. I knew straight away what had happened, even though I never thought for a minute it would. I lay in bed, frozen, and waited for them to come and tell me. It felt like for ever. They came up the stairs together and sat on the end of my bed and told me that Rosie had been found dead that morning. She'd taken tablets with alcohol before she'd gone to bed. She'd choked on her own vomit. There was no note. They thought maybe it was an accident. She hadn't meant to do it. They asked me if I knew anything. I turned my phone on to show them the messages and there was a new one on there. She must have sent it after I turned my phone off. She'd texted me goodbye. She said that she was sorry.' Tears were falling fast now.

'Shit. Florence, that's awful. I'm so sorry.'

She shook her head, not wanting pity. 'I should have realised. I should have replied. I should have known what she was going through and been there for her like she'd been for me, even when I hadn't deserved it. Just a few kind words could've changed everything but I couldn't even do that. I couldn't bring myself to tell her it was okay when I didn't feel okay.' She was angry with herself. Angry for crying. She didn't deserve pity.

'You can't blame yourself, Florence. It wasn't you who made your friend take her own life. You know it's not that simple. She made that choice.'

'I should have known she was unhappy.'

'Hey, you didn't tell her how you were feeling, did you? People hide things and struggle on their own and that's awful but it's not your fault. She wouldn't have even known you'd seen her messages. She probably thought you were asleep. It's sad she couldn't talk to someone sooner but she had parents and family and teachers. It sounds like no one else saw the warning signs either. You can't take responsibility for this.'

'But I feel responsible. You don't have to try and make me feel better. I wouldn't blame you if you judged me. I do. I'm sure my parents do, and Rosie's. They say they don't but how can they not? Ever since then my parents have watched me like a hawk, probably worried I'd do the same. Sometimes I thought about it. I didn't want to worry them but I couldn't help it. I wanted it all to go away. I ended up hurting myself.'

She instinctively held her wrists, hidden by her collection of bracelets. 'That's why they referred me to Manor Lane. I worried them sick. I've put them through so much. They lost someone too and I made it even worse. I don't know how to make it better now. It feels like the damage is done. My mum and dad barely talk to each other. I don't think they even like each other any more. They're probably only still together because they're worried if they split up I'd do something stupid again. Now we're all just treading on eggshells, not talking any more. It's such a mess. All I want to do is go back and fix it.'

'But you can't. You know that. The best thing you can do now is forgive yourself and move on. You made one mistake. You know if you could go back you'd do things differently. You're a good person, Florence. You have to forgive yourself.'

She sighed, grateful but still not able to believe it. 'You sound like Howard.' *It's not your mistakes that make you who you are,* he'd said to her. *It's how you learn from them.*

'Well good, because he knows what he's talking about.'

'I've tried to move on but I just … I feel so guilty. Not just about what happened but about the future, about being happy, and wanting things. Good things.'

'I wish I could make you happy.'

'You do. I think that's part of the problem. Despite everything I've been happy all day. The happiest I've been in ages. Of all days. I feel bad that I've felt so good. I've been thinking about other things when I should be remembering Rosie.'

'It sounds like you'll always remember Rosie. You don't have to feel sad or put your life on hold to do that. Do you think she'd want you to be unhappy?'

'I don't know. She always thought I was the strong one. I wish I was.'

'You can be.'

Jasper shifted so he was sitting close beside her, both of them facing the sea.

Florence rested her head on his shoulder. As she listened to the waves lapping the shoreline she felt calm at last. It was out there now. Jasper knew everything and he didn't seem to judge her. She hadn't dared imagine it was possible. The whole day seemed like a surreal dream. Had she made him up inside her head?

'I know what we should do,' Jasper said. 'We should mark the anniversary. Do something positive that shows Rosie you've not forgotten about her. Would that help?'

She looked at Jasper and smiled. 'Yeah. I think it would, but what?'

'I dunno. What kind of things did she like? What did you enjoy doing together?'

She pictured them both then. Memories flicking through her mind like pictures in a photo album. Camping in the garden, sleepovers, shopping, trying on the most ridiculous, hideous outfits they could find and howling with laughter in the changing rooms. Days out to theme parks, swimming pools, local fetes. Homework, art projects, baking in the kitchen with sweets and sprinkles and runny icing. Christmas plays, Easter egg hunts, summer holidays ... It was the holidays she enjoyed the most. Sitting on the sand with the sound of the sea and the smell of the saltwater it was easy to remember. She'd been remembering ever since they arrived. 'When we were growing up we used to go away every summer. Our families together. We'd stay near a beach and hang out for a week having day trips or just playing on the sand. Every year, even when we were older, we'd spend hours making giant sandcastles. Big piles of sand, decorated with sea shells and driftwood. It became like a tradition. Every year they'd get more elaborate.'

Jasper nodded. 'Why don't we do that then?'

'Yeah, I'd like that.' Jasper was right. It was the perfect thing to do.

Jasper stood up with intent and Florence laughed. 'You mean now?'

'Why not?'

She looked around the empty beach. 'But, it's dark.'

'Are you tired?'

'Not really. Are you?'

'Nope.'

She shrugged the blanket off her shoulders and stood up too. 'Okay then. Let's do it.'

They walked across the sand back to the van. Jasper opened the back door as quietly as he could and they peered inside. Andrew was asleep on the chair by the back door and Wilf had converted the bench seats into a bed and was slumped under a duvet, a cup tilted in one hand and the bottle of vodka he'd bought from the pub leaning on the pillow next to him. When Jasper crept closer his eyes snapped open.

'Wha' you doing?' His voice was thick with sleep and slurred from alcohol.

'Have you got anything like a spade in here?' Jasper whispered.

'Er, nope.'

'What's the closest thing you've got that'll do the job of a spade, then?'

'Spatula.' He pointed to the kitchen unit. 'Wooden spoon? I dunno.' He sat up on his elbows, confusion on his face.

Jasper was already rummaging through the camping box. He took out a head torch then took some wooden spoons from the cupboard drawer.

'Is Florence okay?'

'Yeah mate, she's alright. She's going to be fine. You go back to sleep.'

Wilf slid further down the bed and was snoring before Jasper finished talking.

Jasper removed the bottle and the cup from him, putting them out of reach on the cupboard, then he strapped the torch to his head and handed Florence the wooden spoon.

They stepped out of the van, closing the door quietly, then

Jasper switched on the torch and they followed the beam of light back to the beach.

The pile of sand was the height of Florence's waist. It was decorated with driftwood, shells and stones and looked like an oversized cupcake. Around it they'd dug a channel, like a moat, which was slowly filling with seawater. The tide was coming in, every third or fourth wave leaving wide arcs of wet sand, eating away at the pile before it retreated. In a few hours it would be gone.

Florence picked up a stick from the pile of scavenged items they'd found and started to write in the sand, her arms aching from digging as she formed the letters.

Jasper angled himself so his torch lit up the sand where she was working.

She wrote *For Rosie xx* in big curly letters around the pile on the side furthest from the sea. When she was done she surveyed their work, satisfied, then took out her phone to take a photo.

Jasper lit it up with his torch. 'It's amazing what you can do with two wooden spoons and a plank, don't you think?'

'Yeah. Rosie would have loved this, thank you.' Florence smiled at him. 'You know, you always manage to make me feel better.'

'That's because I'm ninety per cent joyful, I told you. I've got joy to spare.'

He looked at her and she reeled back as the light from his head torch momentarily blinded her.

'Oh, sorry.' He switched it off and they were suddenly shrouded in darkness.

As her eyes adjusted he stepped closer. The nearness of him made her skin prickle with anticipation. Before she realised what was happening his lips were on hers.

She was momentarily stunned. She felt like her breath had left her and her heart had stopped, then suddenly she was alive and breathing him in, her heart racing as she kissed him back.

She'd been longing to do this all day. For weeks. Ever since he first walked in the door at Manor Lane. She'd been so conscious of the space between them that it had felt electrified. All she wanted was to cross that space, to touch his fingers, his face, his body. She pressed herself against him at last, closing as much of the space as she could. She reached up and buried her fingers in his hair and a dazzling light shone in her face. She recoiled again, laughing.

'*Lumos*,' Jasper said, grinning.

'You're blinding me.'

'Sorry. I just like looking at you.' He reached up and traced her chin with his fingers. 'You're so beautiful.'

'Stop it. I'm not. And you look like a lighthouse.'

He laughed and took it off, roughing his hair back up then planted another firm, confident kiss on her lips like it was a totally normal thing to do. 'I've been wanting to do that for ages.'

'Me too.

'You should have said.'

'I couldn't. I didn't think you'd like me. I thought you'd go for someone prettier. Nicer.'

'Ridiculous. You're perfect. I fancied you from day one.'

'I wish you'd told me.'

'I couldn't. That tiny ten per cent kept holding me back. I thought you'd want someone manlier. More intelligent.'

'Not me.'

'We should talk more.'

'Theme of the day: it's good to talk.' They were grinning at each other. Florence used to think there was nothing she liked more than talking to Jasper. Now she'd got a taste of him there were things she wanted to do even more.

'Come on.' He took her hand and together they walked back up the beach. They found a spot where the sand was higher and there was no danger of the tide reaching them and then they sunk down onto the beach and wrapped themselves in each other, as the sea slowly claimed their creation.

Chapter Eighteen

Florence woke up to the sound of seagulls. She was lying on Jasper's chest, his arm around her. Their legs were entwined, her feet were cold and there was sand between her toes. She shivered and Jasper's arms tightened around her. He kissed the top of her head.

'Morning.'

She looked up and he kissed her mouth, his hands cupping her face.

Memories of the night before came flooding back and her skin tingled. It no longer mattered whether he could tell what she was thinking.

He pulled away from her and studied her face. 'This is nice.'

She smiled. 'It is.'

'My arm's gone dead though.'

'Oh, sorry.' She sat up and looked at the beach where their sand pile had been. Only a few stones and pieces of driftwood remained. The tide was going out again, the waves lapping further from them now.

The sun was still low, giving the sky a soft pink glow. Birds circled above the castle on the other side of the estuary. There was a fishing boat passing, heading out to sea.

Florence took her phone out of her back pocket to take a picture and switched it on. There was a text from Kimi.

Hey, how's it going? Thinking of you today xx

Kimi probably hadn't got much sleep either, what with Jess and the others staying at hers. She took a photo of the beach with the castle in the background and sent it to her in reply then followed it with a smiley face.

The time on the screen said it was five in the morning. 'God, it's early. I didn't even know the sun was up at five o'clock.' She rubbed her face and ran her tongue across her teeth. She wanted to shower and freshen up but she didn't want to wake Andrew and Wilf by getting stuff out of the van. She looked around. The van was still in the car park, doors shut, no one else around.

'You want to sleep some more?' she said to Jasper. They could only have had a few hours.

'I can think of lots of things I'd rather do.' He pulled her into his lap and made a noise like a growl.

Florence bent down to kiss him again. There was a sudden rush of noise. She looked up and saw that the doors of the van were now open and Andrew was crossing the sand towards them, followed by an irritated, half-asleep Wilf.

Andrew looked wide awake. He held his iPad out at them. 'Guys, I know where Howard lives.' He dropped down beside them, oblivious to the fact that Florence was sitting in Jasper's lap. 'Megan messaged me. She remembered what she'd read about Margot. It was an interview in the local paper.'

Wilf arrived behind Andrew and looked at Jasper and Florence in annoyance. 'Great, so you two got it on last night. Andrew's got himself a new girlfriend. What the fuck is wrong with me?' He gestured at himself like he was some kind of catch but ended up pointing at a ketchup stain on his T-shirt.

Andrew looked impatiently at Wilf. 'Megan's not my girlfriend. She's gay.'

Wilf's eyes widened. 'Seriously? Wow, what a waste. Bad luck, mate.'

'I'm sure her girlfriend doesn't think it's a waste and anyway, I don't see how it's bad luck. I don't want a girlfriend.'

Wilf's eyes grew even wider. 'You want a boyfriend?'

'No! I've told you before, I don't want that sort of relation-ship with anyone. I just want a friend. Megan is my friend. Can we get back to the point?'

Wilf blinked and looked around the beach. 'Yeah, what was that?'

Andrew tapped the iPad screen. 'You need to see this. Megan sent me a link. It's an interview with Margot. It was done at her house. There are some photos. That one is Margot standing in her garden. You can see her house in the background. See? It's pink.'

Florence thought of all the houses she'd seen in Borth y Castell, built on the hillside and looking out to sea. Nearly all of them were white.

'And what's more . . . ' He scrolled further down. 'There's the view from her front garden. You can see the harbour by the car park where we first arrived. Which means if you can see it from her house, we can see her house from the harbour.'

Florence studied the picture. She could see the harbour through a row of pine trees. It was south of the house and not far below. 'Okay, so we just need to go and stand at the harbour and look up at the hillside on the right?'

'Yes. We should easily be able to pick out a house that colour.' Andrew took the iPad back and scrambled to his feet.

'Hey, hold up, we're not going now. I need at least three hours more kip.'

Andrew looked at Wilf, incredulous. 'Don't be ridiculous. How can you possibly sleep now?'

Florence slid back onto the sand and reached for her socks and shoes. 'We could just go and have a look, work out where it is. We can't go knocking on the door at this time in the morning anyway.'

'Why not?' Andrew looked as though he might explode with frustration.

'Hold the phone already,' Wilf said. 'We're not turning up at stupid o'clock and getting Howard out of bed. He's hardly going to thank us for that, is he? And I'm going nowhere without at least having breakfast.'

Andrew scanned the three of them, confused.

'I'll go with you, Andrew,' Florence said, standing up. 'We can see where it is, come back here, get some breakfast and then walk up a bit later if it's not too far.'

'I'll come with you,' Jasper said.

'Yeah well, take your time,' Wilf said while yawning. 'If I don't get more zeds I'm literally going to die.'

Andrew opened his mouth to correct him but Wilf just held up a hand, gave him a death stare and turned back to the van.

Jasper and Florence followed Andrew along the coastal path towards the first car park. Florence was smiling. She couldn't believe how much she'd been dreading this day yet now it was here she realised it wasn't that different from any other day. It didn't hurt any more or less. She still missed Rosie. She still had this awful regret that would probably never quite leave her, but she'd also crossed a milestone. She'd made it through the year, and she was hopeful for the next one. She was looking forward to telling Howard that. She wanted to thank him for sticking with her.

The trees opened out onto the main car park. They

crossed it and walked down the steps to the beach, then they orientated themselves so they were looking in the direction they figured Margot's house must be. There were fewer buildings on that side. They were bigger than the town houses and more spread out, with large windows and balconies designed to make the most of the view.

'It's got to be that one,' Andrew said, his eyes flitting from a house on the hill to his iPad. 'It's the same colour, and it's got the same octagonal turret.'

Jasper studied the picture. 'Yes, you're right.'

Florence stood further back, taking in the house. It was large and impressive. Like a castle in miniature. There was a driveway and garage to the side of the house, just visible through the pine trees.

She held her hand up to shield her eyes from the rising sun and looked again. 'That's it. That's the house, and if I'm not mistaken that's Howard's car in the drive.'

'Wilf, wake up!' Andrew shook him again and he half opened his eyes, raised his head from the pillow then slumped back down and closed them again. 'No.'

'Wilf, it's important.'

'I'm asleep.'

'You're not, you're talking to me.'

'Piss off for an hour and come back when I've had bacon.'

'Wilf, we can see Margot Green's house and Howard's car's in the drive.'

'Good. Well done.'

'C'mon Wilf, we should go. We've waited an hour and I can't wait any longer. Megan's on her way too. She'll be here any minute.'

'Dude, it's a Sunday morning. He, like most people, would probably appreciate a lie in.'

'Wilf! We've come all this way. We've been worried about him. We need answers. It's time to go.'

Wilf exhaled heavily, sat fully upright and reached for his T-shirt, then he breathed into his hand and sniffed it, recoiling. 'Alright. Is it walking distance? Cos I'm probably still over the limit and I'm not risking getting stopped with this breath.'

'We can walk, it's not far,' Florence said.

'Okay, okay, breakfast first.'

Andrew made a noise of frustration and stormed out of the van.

'For God's sake.' Wilf swung his legs off the bed and reached for his jeans. 'Howard better be alright and coming back soon because Andrew is not done with his therapy yet.'

They walked up the steep hill to the house, Andrew leading the way.

Wilf stopped to get his breath back, resting his hands on his hips and gasping for breath. 'How is Andrew going so fast? He never does any exercise. He's like a bloody mountain goat.'

Florence stopped too, looking back at how far they'd

come. The sea was sparkling below them. Her phone buzzed and she took it out of her pocket, checking the screen. It was a message from Kimi and a warning that her battery was low. She went to open the message but it buzzed again and the screen went blank. 'Damn it.' She wouldn't be able to charge it until she got back to the van.

'You okay?' Jasper said, dropping back and taking her hand.

'Yeah, fine.' She put her phone away and smiled. The easy way he touched her now kept catching her by surprise. She'd get a short burst of electricity, leaving her hyper alert and aware of him, her mind unable to settle on anything else.

They walked the rest of the way together in comfortable silence, and it was only when they reached the end of Margot's drive that Florence focussed on why they'd come.

Andrew rang the doorbell and stood back, staring at it expectantly. The house stayed silent and Andrew stepped forward to try again. 'Patience,' Megan warned him, just as the door swung open.

A girl appeared before them in the doorway, her expression questioning. She was nearly as tall as Andrew, despite being barefoot, and looked a similar age to them, maybe a year or two older. She was wearing frayed shorts and an asymmetrical tank top. Her hair was blonde and wavy with a pink dip dye and her eyes were made up with heavy winged eyeliner. When she pushed her hair back from her face Florence noticed a tattoo of a flower on her wrist. 'You want to see Margot, right?' she said, as though this were both normal and not very interesting.

'Actually, we're here to see Howard Green,' Andrew said.

The girl raised an eyebrow then stood back and called over her shoulder, 'Dad? There's some people here for you.'

The four of them shared a brief look of surprise. Florence's mind worked quickly, trying to readjust to the concept of Howard as a father.

There were footsteps in the hallway then Howard appeared in front of them. He looked much the same as he always did but more tired. 'Guys, what are you doing here? Are you okay?'

'We've been looking for you,' Andrew said. 'The staff at Manor Lane made it sound like you might not be coming back. We were worried something was wrong.'

Howard rubbed his chin and contemplated them all with concern, his attention momentarily taken by the bruise on Jasper's cheek.

'It was his idea,' Wilf said, pointing at Andrew. 'I'm just the driver.'

'We heard the staff say you were with your sister so I found her online,' Andrew said.

'We all wanted to see you,' Jasper said.

Megan held up a hand in greeting. 'And I'm Megan. I'm here for Andrew.'

'She's my friend,' Andrew said proudly.

'Okay, I think you need to come in.' Howard stepped back and gestured inside.

Chapter Nineteen

They walked into a large farmhouse style kitchen. 'Do your parents know you're here?'

'Not exactly,' Jasper said. 'It was kind of a spur of the moment thing.'

'It's okay though, they're not worried,' Florence said. 'They just think we're doing something else.'

Andrew nodded in agreement.

Howard gestured to a rustic table in the middle of the room. It had bench seats on two sides and a chair at the end with a newspaper spread out in front of it, as though Howard had been sitting reading it before he'd been disturbed. They sat down obediently.

Howard's daughter was lingering at the door. When she noticed them looking at her curiously she said, 'I'll leave you guys to it,' and disappeared.

Wilf looked disappointed.

'This is my fault,' Howard said. 'I should have

explained better when I left. I shouldn't have kept you hanging like that, I'm sorry.' He placed half a dozen mugs on the table.

'Is everything okay?' Florence said. 'Are you okay?'

'Yes, Florence, thank you for asking. We're all fine.' He sat down on the chair. 'It's just been a challenging week. Sometimes things happen and family have to take priority.'

Florence nodded but Jasper, Andrew and Wilf continued to stare at him, waiting for more.

He gestured to the door where the girl had just been standing. 'My daughter, Harriet. She's not been having such a good time lately. She needed me here. She lives with my ex-wife, Jana, usually. I try to see her most weekends. She's doing her second year of A levels and I'm sure you know what it's like: school pressure, social lives, making choices. It's not always easy. Sometimes it gets too much.'

'So, she came here to get away from things?' Andrew said.

Howard looked like he was choosing his words carefully. 'She's always been close to my sister, Margot, so I was fairly certain she'd turn up here.'

Florence understood then. Harriet had run away. That's why he left so quickly, and why he looked so tired. He must have been worried sick. 'Is she okay? Harriet, I mean?'

'Yes, we're getting there, I think. She might need some time out. Maybe a change of direction. She's got plenty of options. I think she sees that now and that's what's import-ant. As I've said to you all many times, there's help if you ask

221

for it. Unfortunately it's not always easy to admit you need help, even to your parents.'

'*Especially* your parents,' Wilf said. 'They're not all as understanding as you.'

'Well, I'm not perfect, Wilf. We all make mistakes. I'm sure Harriet would agree with that. I think sometimes we expect our parents to be mind readers. Even studying theory of the mind can't teach you to do that.'

Wilf shifted uncomfortably in his seat and stared at the table.

Andrew perked up then. 'So, now you know that Harriet is okay, when are you coming back to Manor Lane? Can we have our Tuesday appointment?'

Howard looked at him with an expression of regret but Andrew continued to stare hopefully at him.

'Okay, listen. I think we've all got some unfinished business we should cover. How about we have a cup of tea and I speak to you all individually. You've travelled a long way. You're probably hungry too. I can get Margot to fix you some breakfast if you like?'

Howard introduced them all to Margot then asked Jasper to join him outside. Florence watched them talking through the French doors while Margot busied herself in the kitchen, popping slices of bread in a toaster then putting plates, butter and jam on the table. She seemed a little flustered by the strangers sharing her kitchen and was fretting that she wouldn't have enough to feed them all.

'Really, we don't want to be any trouble,' Megan insisted.

'Oh, it's no bother. I just wish I'd known you were coming. Honestly, I've gone from not seeing anyone from one day to the next to a full house this week. Fortunately I got some bits in for Harriet yesterday.' She rooted around in a cupboard then added peanut butter and a plate of assorted biscuits to the table. 'I did have some Hobnobs somewhere but I think Harriet squirrelled them up to her room. They always were her favourite.'

Wilf nodded approvingly and helped himself to a chocolate finger.

'In fact,' Margot continued, 'I don't think she's had any breakfast yet. I'll just go and see if she wants to join us.

As soon as Margot was out of earshot Florence looked at the others and whispered, 'I can't believe Howard has a daughter. Did you know? I didn't know. Why do you think he never mentioned her?'

Andrew and Wilf both shrugged.

'Maybe he likes to keep his private life private,' Megan said.

'Maybe he wants to hide her away from the likes of us,' Wilf said. 'Did you see her? She's a fox!'

Florence frowned at him. 'Do you have to?' she hissed.

He pulled an expression of innocence. 'What?'

Margot walked back into the kitchen. 'She says she'll be down in a minute.'

Florence gave Wilf a warning look then smiled at Margot.

'At least her appetite's returning.' Margot took the toast out of the toaster and added some more bread to it. 'Young people do worry me. So much stress and pressure these days, and Harriet's always so hard on herself. As if life's not hard enough already. I wish everyone would just relax a bit. Life's a marathon, not a sprint, as my mum used to say. Mind you, I'm probably too much the other way. If everyone was like me no one would ever get anything done.'

'Hey, you've written three books. That's an amazing achievement,' Megan said.

Margot waved a dismissive hand. 'It took me ten years to write those. I've been saying the next one's almost done for years.'

'You're writing another *Dragons of Bryn* book?' Florence asked.

'No, it's a fantasy novel, for older readers this time. My publisher gave me the go ahead about five years ago but it's taken me so long they've probably given up on me now.'

'Are you kidding?' Megan said. 'You're totally popular. Think of all those parents reading your books to their kids. They'd love it if you wrote something for them. I know I would. I read them to my brother before he could read them himself. You're a legend in our house.'

Margot smiled modestly. 'Really?'

'Absolutely. You have to see this.' She scrolled through her phone then held it up for Margot to see. A video was playing. 'That's my brother on World Book Day just last March.'

Margot wiped her hands on a tea towel and watched the screen, transfixed. 'He's Gruffydd?'

'Yep. Loves him. His friends too. They'd go nuts if they knew I'd met you today. In fact ...' She turned her phone around and pointed it at herself, angling it so Margot was behind her. 'Can I have a selfie? Just to prove it's really you.'

Margot peered at the camera and winced. 'Goodness, really?'

Megan grinned at the camera then checked the photo. 'They're going to be so jealous when they see this.'

Margot looked like she couldn't quite believe what Megan was saying.

'Seriously, Margot, you're super popular. Have you seen the reviews you get?'

'No, the papers haven't reviewed me for years.'

'Not in the newspapers, on Amazon and Goodreads. Look.' She tapped into her phone and held it up again. '4.7 out of five stars. "My nine-year-old loves these stories so much she's read them until the pages dropped out." And look, "funny, charming tales and just scary enough to make them exciting page turners. My niece was captivated." Have you really never seen this stuff?' She scrolled through countless others.

'No, never. I've never used my computer as anything more than a word processor. Howard bought me a tablet for Christmas but I only use it to look up facts or check the weather.'

'There's fan art too.'

'What's fan art?'

Megan tapped again and scrolled through the images on her phone.

Margot's eyes widened. 'Wow. Who drew all these?'

'Your fans, Margot. Do you see now? People love your books.'

Margot was staring at the images, speechless, as more and more came up, then she reeled back with her hand over her mouth. 'Oh!'

'Sorry.' Megan hastily closed the screen, trying to hide a smile. 'People do like to get a bit creative with the script sometimes.'

'I really don't think I want to see Dafi doing . . .'

'Aled. Yeah, you're right, bad example, but you see what I mean? It really is worth checking out the internet. You've got some seriously loyal fans out there.'

'Imagine how many more you could have if you updated your website too,' Andrew said. 'The fact people are even finding your books proves the value of word of mouth.'

'Oh, is there something wrong with my website?'

As Andrew proceeded to list the faults with Margot's current site Jasper returned to the kitchen. He smiled reassuringly at Florence then nodded to Wilf. 'You're next.'

Andrew made a noise of impatience as he watched Wilf put a slice of buttered toast in his mouth and stand up.

*

Jasper didn't touch the food on the table. Not even the chocolate biscuits.

Florence kept glancing at him as the conversation continued around them. Harriet had joined them and they continued to discuss Margot and her lack of experience with the internet. Megan and Harriet were giving her a lesson on Twitter and Instagram and were attempting to explain what memes and GIFs were while Margot listened with an expression of morbid fascination, laughing at the examples Megan was pulling up on her phone. It was the kind of conversation Jasper would usually find impossible to ignore. It was brimming with potential humour. Instead, his foot tapped the floor making the bench seat wobble and he watched the conversation rather than listened to it.

'Are you okay?' Florence whispered eventually.

'Yeah.' He looked at her then added, 'You want to go outside for a bit?'

'Sure.'

They walked out onto the front drive, not wanting to disturb Howard and Wilf in the garden.

The view of the sea was just visible through the trees and they walked towards it, instinctively holding hands. On the path opposite the house was a bench seat that offered an uninterrupted view of the coastline. They went to it and sat down, silent for a moment, then Florence said, 'So, what's up?'

Jasper looked unusually glum. 'I dunno. I guess talking to Howard just made me think about going home. It's kind of bringing out the ten per cent in me.'

'You're feeling anxious?'

'Yeah.' He swallowed hard, his eyes fixed on the view.

She held his hand in both of hers. She wanted to tell him not to be scared but she knew it was as meaningless as telling someone in the depths of despair to cheer up. 'Can I help?' she said instead.

He put an arm around her. 'You are helping. I just wish this weekend could go on for ever.'

'Why can't it?'

'Well, because we have to go home, and I have to see my mum and sort things out.'

'Have you heard from her since you left?'

'Yeah. She texted to say sorry before we even got to Cambridge. She's tried to call a few times but I've kept my phone on silent. She left a voice message saying she's not been herself lately and she wants to get help. She promised it'll never happen again.'

'Well, that's good. Do you believe her?'

'I guess. She's said that sort of thing before, but then she's never hit me before. She gets angry, it's pretty intense, but it's never been directed at me. I know she'll be feeling awful about it. I don't want to her to feel bad, but I just don't think I can let it go that quickly.'

'Understandable. Do you think you'll be okay?'

'I hope so. Howard's going to call her. She's always listened to him.'

'So, why do you still look worried?'

'I dunno.' He was sitting hunched up and still staring at the sea. 'Maybe because I don't just want me to be okay. I want us to be okay.'

'Us?' Florence had never really noticed the word before. Now it sounded technicolour. An explosion of dancing light. 'How do you mean?'

'Well, what if when we get home things are different with us? I mean, this weekend has been so great. I want it to always be like that, but I know it won't be.' He shifted so that he was turned to her, but he could hardly catch her eye. 'You should know. I'm not always this person. I can be embarrassing and annoying and say the wrong thing. I have days when I realise I'm not funny or smart or brave and all I want to do is hide at home. It's like I have a voice in my head telling me I'm an embarrassing non-entity that shouldn't be allowed in public.'

'Hey, don't say that. You're not. Not ever. You're none of those things.'

'But it still feels like it. They're my Phantom Menace days, that's what I call them. When I'm Jar Jar Binks in a world full of Jedis, sprinkling midi-chlorians on the magic of the force.'

She knew exactly what he meant. 'We all have days like that. You've seen enough of mine. That's the good thing about us. We've seen the worst of each other and we're still here. I'm still here.'

He swallowed hard. 'You might get fed up with me.'

'No, Jasper. Those are the days when I want to see you the most. Those are the days when I'll be your personal cheerleader. I'll keep telling you how amazing you are until you believe me.' She took his hand and squeezed it. 'What happened to Jasper the optimist?'

'I know. It's just dawned on me that I've not had much to lose before. The thought of losing you now is scary.'

'Don't think about it then. Think about the good things. Think about keeping me.' She mimicked his most persuasive, most flirtatious smile.

'Wow. My mind's just gone totally blank.'

'Maybe this will help.' She leaned over and kissed him, her lips lingering on his.

Jasper's eyes were closed. He opened them slowly, focussing on Florence, then said in a husky, broken voice, 'Hmm, I dunno, how about we try that again?'

Back in the kitchen Harriet was talking to Megan and Margot while Andrew sat staring impatiently at the French doors. Florence looked outside and saw Howard pacing as he talked on his phone and Wilf walking back to the house.

'About time too,' Andrew muttered as Wilf stepped inside. He stood with his hands in his pockets, his face pale and his expression humourless.

'Are you okay?' Jasper said.

'Yeah. Howard called my dad. My brother's been arrested.'

Florence put her hand over her mouth. 'Oh no! Are you going to be in any trouble?'

'I dunno. I don't think so. At least not with Dad or the police. It sounds like Dad just wants me at home. He's not happy, obviously. He'll be even less happy when I tell him I've decided I'm not going back to my mechanics course, but right now I think going to catering college beats going to prison on the list of things likely to piss off your parent. At least it should anyway.'

'Yes, and at least if your brother's in jail he can't kill you,' Andrew said.

'Thank you, Andrew, for those kind words of comfort.' Wilf joined them at the table and sat next to Florence. 'You're next up to see Howard, by the way. He's just talking to your parents.'

Florence's stomach swooped and she sprang out of her seat. 'Howard called my parents?'

'No, they called him while we were talking. It sounded like they were on their way over.'

Howard was putting his phone back in his pocket when Florence stepped out into the garden. She walked straight up to him and stood with her hands on her hips, waiting for an explanation.

Howard dipped his head and looked at her seriously. 'Everything okay, Florence?'

'No, my parents are coming? Why are my parents coming?'

'Well, I imagine they've been worried about you. You hadn't told them you were coming here apparently.'

'Why didn't they just call me?' She remembered her phone battery was flat and sighed. 'I could have told them they don't need to come. I was doing alright. This has been good for me. Now I feel like I've let them down and they're going to be annoyed with me. I've just gone from feeling good to guilty.'

'They're not annoyed, Florence, they just wanted to know you're okay. I don't think they even knew you were with me. Your mum said she knew you were with the others and wanted to know if I'd heard anything about it. She was surprised when I said you were here. I told her you seemed fine and I asked if she wanted to speak to you but she said she'd rather just come. She said it was important and they were already on their way.'

'What?' Florence shook her head, bewildered. If they were already on their way they must have had a good idea where she was but how did they know? She'd deliberately told Kimi she was going to Wales, not whereabouts in Wales. It dawned on her that they might have spoken to Wilf's dad, and the thought made her feel sick. That meant they'd also know about the trouble with his brother. She dreaded to think how her parents would've reacted to that. 'Oh God.' She sat down on the wall, defeated. They were bound to be upset to just set off like that. They never did anything impulsive.

'Florence, everything's okay. Your parents care about you. You need to start opening up to them more. Trusting them.'

'Yeah well, like you said, it's not always that easy when it's your parents.' She thought about their conversation in the kitchen then looked at Howard, curious. 'Why did you never mention you have a daughter?'

He looked almost guilty. 'Do you think I should have done?'

'It might have helped to know that you have a daughter the same age as us, who gets stressed and has issues just like we do. It kind of makes us all seem a bit more normal, you know?'

'Yes, I see your point.' He stretched his legs out and folded his arms as though this was an interesting topic of conversation, like the many they'd had in his office. 'It's actually a subject that's often debated in therapy. How much should a therapist reveal about their own life? There's an argument for sharing enough to help patients to recognise that everyone can have failings and difficulties. There's also an argument for remaining neutral and being a blank mirror for a patient to project onto. I think what I've tended towards is using self-involving disclosures rather than self-revealing, which means I prefer to share my personal reactions and thoughts on subjects, rather than personal details which could potentially involve other people.'

Florence felt a flash of irritation. Was everything he did so contrived? She'd thought he spoke to them like individuals. Like he was really interested in them as people. What if this wasn't the case at all? What if he was actually just going through the motions, saying what he thought they needed to hear? She remembered Wilf saying he was just a guy who was paid to ask questions and tears pricked in her eyes as she wondered for the first time if he was right.

Howard watched her thoughtfully for a moment, then nodded, as though he understood what she was thinking. 'Okay. Maybe there's more to it than that,' he said, taking his time. 'Maybe, despite being immensely proud of Harriet and the person she's become, it's a part of my life that I'm not particularly proud of myself for. I see young people all the time affected by broken relationships and absent parents. I never wanted that for my family. It's hard to admit that I know I could have done more. Perhaps that's how I'm supposed to feel? How all parents feel? All I know is every problem your child faces can feel like a failing in yourself to protect them. When they hurt, you hurt. Maybe that's why we're often the hardest people to talk to.'

She understood then. He was a person. A person like everyone else. He didn't always have the right answers but that was okay. In fact, it was kind of reassuring. 'Okay, I understand. I will try to talk to my parents more.'

'Good.' He smiled. 'You're a very interesting person to talk to. Let them know the real you.'

'Maybe.' She looked at her hands, suddenly shy and keen to change the subject. 'Howard, I've been wondering. What was the book you were going to give me this weekend? The one you said I might find interesting?'

He perked up. 'Ah, you're right. I'd forgotten about that. I actually have it with me. It was in my bag when I came up here. Wait there a minute.'

He got up and walked back to the house. When he returned he was holding a large, hardback reference book. He put it in her hands.

'For the Love of Words,' Florence read.

'It's about linguistics. The study of language. It's been on my shelf for years. I thought you might appreciate it.'

She flicked through the pages, her eyes drawn to the sub titles: Dialect, Morphology, Phonetics, Semantics and Pragmatics, the Bouba-Kiki Effect, Synaesthesia.

Howard put a finger on the page titled 'synaesthesia'. 'It was this one that I thought you'd find particularly interesting.'

'Synaesthesia?' She wrinkled up her nose. She didn't know the word and she wasn't sure she liked it. It sounded sticky, like fly paper.

'It's where your senses cross over. Some people taste words or see sounds or letters look like colours. It's not fully understood, and everyone's experience is different. It's just a subject I thought you might find interesting.'

Her eyes widened. She scanned the pages wanting to take in all the words at once. This she could relate to. This was why she saw words as patterns and pictures. 'This is a thing?'

'It is a thing.'

'I get this.'

'I thought you might.'

'Is it a bad thing? Like, a condition?'

He laughed. 'No, Florence, it's not bad thing, it's just different. Different is good. Some say it's a gift. A super power if you like. It can give you a whole different perspective on the world.'

'Oh, I don't think I have that.'

'Well, take it home and have a read. See what you think. You're very interested in words and language. I think you'll find it all interesting, and the more you understand language, the more you'll be able to use it to your advantage in your writing. I know you enjoy writing.'

'I do,' she said, still staring at the words.

Howard crossed his legs and leant on the back of the seat. 'So, it's been an interesting weekend, and today is a meaningful day for you. You want to tell me more about it?'

Florence told Howard about their journey to Wales, about Andrew meeting Chris Hadfield and having his bag stolen, about Wilf's brother's hidden package and Andrew meeting Megan and how he and Wilf seemed to have found a genuine friendship disguised under a layer of mutual banter.

She described how the feelings she'd been trying to escape had caught up with her anyway, that she'd told Jasper about Rosie and how he'd helped her draw both a metaphorical and an actual line in the sand. She didn't tell him about the change in her relationship with Jasper but it must have been obvious from the look on her face. Every time his name came up she found herself grinning.

'This all sounds very positive, Florence.'

'I guess.'

'So what's next for you, do you think?'

She thought about Monday with a mixture of feelings. She shared some of Jasper's fears but she was excited too. She wanted to take everything she'd learnt in the last year and use it to keep getting better. She wanted to start making plans. Before she could do that, however, she was going to have to face her parents.

Florence's notebook

Life Lessons to Remember

1. *Don't compare your life story to other people's edited highlights.*
2. *Don't blame the person you are now for the person you used to be.*
3. *True friendship comes when you can reveal your true self.*
4. *Keep seeking out the positives: the helpers, the carers, the solutions, the hope, the curiosity, all the little things that make you smile. Store them up and remember them on the days too dark to see.*
5. *There is always a moment in the future you'll be glad you stuck around for.*

Chapter Twenty

They stayed in the kitchen while Andrew took his turn talking to Howard in the garden. Margot stood at the sink washing up and Florence and Jasper helped by drying the dishes. Wilf, Megan and Harriet sat at the table, making small talk. Wilf was leading a debate on favourite TV snack and making them both laugh with his strongly held views on people who eat crisps in the cinema. Florence was waiting to pick the right time to tell Jasper that her parents were on their way but she kept holding back, not wanting to admit their weekend was going to come to an end sooner than they'd hoped. Jasper must have noticed she was quiet because he nudged her, asking what she was thinking. She opened her mouth, debating whether or not to tell him, when there was a sudden shout from the garden. Everyone stopped what they were doing and looked through the glass doors. Andrew and Howard were no longer anywhere to be seen. Moments later the front door opened and Howard walked into the kitchen.

'Andrew's taken off,' he said, rubbing his temple and briefly closing his eyes. 'He's quite upset with me, I'm afraid.'

Wilf stood up. 'We'll go,' he said, looking at Florence and Jasper. They nodded and Megan stood up too.

'Which way did he go?' Florence said.

'Up the hill. The road leads to a car park and nature reserve.'

'Any chickens, pigeons, cats, general wildlife?' Wilf asked.

'I guess,' said Harriet. 'There are ducks on the lake.'

'Come on then.' Wilf grabbed his phone and led the way.

They walked quickly up the hill, Wilf muttering under his breath. 'Just brilliant. Why does he have to pull this shit now? I was actually making some progress there.'

'I think Andrew's got more on his mind than your love life, Wilf,' Florence snapped.

'Well, maybe he should put his friends first. It's been ages since I've had a decent crack at a girl like that.'

Florence stopped in her tracks and stared at Wilf. 'Do you have to talk like that right now?'

'What?'

'Andrew's upset and all you're bothered about is chatting up Howard's daughter.'

'Florence, keep your bra on. There's no harm in looking. I'm a red-blooded male, I can't just switch this off.' He gestured to himself as though he was some kind of prize.

Florence pointed angrily at his puffed up chest. 'For the

record, you're not such a great catch, Wilf. You talk like an alpha male but you're just a boy. If you don't respect women you'll never earn it back. You'll end up lonely and sad with a meal for one watching women on the telly like they're a puzzle you'll never be able to solve.'

Wilf winced. 'Wow. Thanks, Florence.' He started walking again with his head down.

Florence dropped back to walk with Jasper and Megan. 'I didn't mean to say that. He just . . . He gets to me sometimes.'

'Hey, it's fair comment. He needed to be told, and he's more likely to listen to you than any of us,' Jasper said.

'Me? Why me?'

'Come on, think about it: he's got no women around him; his mum's left, he's got no girlfriend, no sister, no female friends to speak of. You're probably one of the few women who actually give him the time of day.'

'Oh. I hadn't really thought about it like that.' She remembered what Wilf had said about his dad being lonely. He was desperate not to end up like that yet she'd just told him that's exactly how it was going to be. She hurried to catch up with him. 'Wilf, I'm sorry, I didn't mean it. Not like that anyway. I just wish you'd talk about women like they were more than what they looked like, you know?'

'For your information, Florence, I like Harriet because she seems edgy and creative and she laughs at my jokes. I don't see why that's so bad.'

'It's not, Wilf. It's not bad.'

'The other stuff, it's just talk. Bravado. You know it's not really me.'

'In that case, you should try being yourself more often. I think women will like you more for it.' Florence waited for him to make some over-confident comment about her flirting with him but instead he gave her a shy smile and said, 'Yeah, well, I'll bear it in mind.'

The road gradually petered out into a dirt track at the top of the hill and branched off into an almost empty car park.

Jasper gave up trying to call Andrew's mobile and called out his name instead. He was answered only by the wind rustling in the canopy of trees above them.

'He won't have gone far,' Florence said. 'He never does.'

'I think I see him,' Wilf said, pointing through a row of conifers. There was a lake just visible on the other side. Florence could make out a wooden jetty leading out into the water and sitting on the end, legs dangling over the side, was a tall, slim, hunched figure.

The four of them walked silently to the end of the jetty and sat down to join Andrew. It was cooler out by the exposed water. A light breeze roughed the surface of the lake and a cluster of swans paddled towards them on the off chance they'd brought food.

Andrew watched them glumly. 'Howard's not coming back,' he said eventually.

'Yeah. I guess we always knew that was a possibility,' Florence said.

'Harriet needs him, apparently.'

'Well, she is his daughter. Family come first and all that.'

'He's moving to Manchester.' He said this like it was completely unthinkable.

'Dude, you'll be okay,' Wilf said. 'Howard's just a bloke. I've said that all along. A decent bloke, but just a bloke. You don't need him to be alright.'

'I can vouch for that. I had a brilliant therapist,' Megan said. 'There are others out there.'

'I don't need therapy,' Andrew said.

'Because you're better?' Florence said. 'You feel like you can manage on your own now?'

'No. Not that.'

'No offence, buddy, but there's a reason why you were referred to Manor Lane. We've all been there. There's no shame in it.'

Andrew shook his head. 'Not me. Not this time.'

Wilf looked at him sceptically. 'What are you on about?'

'Six years ago I was diagnosed with ASD at Manor Lane and I met Howard. It was the first place I ever felt like I fitted in. Howard was the first person who'd ever been genuinely interested in what I had to say. I just ... I wanted to come back.'

'I thought they were reassessing you for OCD?' Jasper said.

'They are, but I don't have it. I like schedules and routines but I don't have OCD.'

'So, what, you pretended you did, just so you could come back?' Florence was surprised; Andrew was usually so honest.

'Not exactly. My parents are pretty persistent. They noticed my college work was starting to be affected and I seemed anxious. They came to their own conclusions. I just didn't put them straight.'

'I don't understand, Andrew,' Florence said. 'Surely if your grades were suffering and you wanted to go back to Manor Lane something must be wrong?'

Andrew was wringing his hands together, still staring at the swans. 'I suppose . . . ' He took a deep breath and continued, his voice unsteady. 'I think maybe I got scared. I can be such an idiot sometimes. I'm always getting things wrong. I started to think, what if I'm not good enough? What if I don't get the grades for uni? I'm worried I'll mess up and no one will want me. I'm scared I'm going to fail.'

All four of them protested at once.

'What?'

'Don't be ridiculous!'

'Of course you won't!'

'Andrew, you're the cleverest person I know.'

He shook his head firmly. 'I'm not. Not really. I like facts, that's all. I have a good memory but I'm not creative. I'm not wise. I'm not even very likeable.'

Florence squeezed Andrew's arm and he stiffened but he didn't move away. 'Andrew. We all like you. That's why we're here now.'

Megan nodded. 'It's true. I liked you the minute you walked in our shop. You're being way too hard on yourself. You've not had much opportunity to be creative yet, it's what you do next that'll give you that chance, and wisdom comes with time and experience.'

Florence nodded in agreement. 'And you're not supposed to think you're perfect. Imagine if you did? You'd be anything but. One of the things I like most about you is that you have this confidence in the things you say but you're never egotistical. Never arrogant. You just like sharing what you know.'

'And how long have you been a Manor Lane?' Wilf said. 'Because I've got to say you seem to have done a good job of making friends. There's no way I would have agreed to spend a whole weekend in a van with a person I didn't like.'

'Think of it this way,' Jasper said, patting him on the shoulder. 'You were never unlikeable. You just hadn't met the right people until now.'

Andrew brushed away fresh tears with the back of his hand and smiled briefly at them all. 'Thank you.'

When they arrived back at Margot's house Florence's heart sank. Her parents' car was parked in the driveway.

The front door opened immediately and her mum crossed the driveway and swept her into a hug. 'We've been so worried about you. Disappearing like that and not telling us where you were and on this day of all days. We've been beside ourselves.'

Florence's dad stood on the drive with his hands in his pockets. He gave his wife a stern look and she stopped talking and hugged her again. The others filed into the house to give them some privacy.

'Mum, I'm okay. I'm fine, really.' She managed to extract herself. 'I didn't mean to worry you. I just wanted to get away and think about something else. I didn't want all the fuss and you watching me and stressing out and . . . '

'You could have told us. We would have understood. We could have arranged to do it properly, come with you.'

'What?'

'It's a lovely thing to do. Really thoughtful.'

'Oh, I don't know, Howard—'

'Yes, why is Howard here?' Her mum was looking at the house in confusion. 'I thought you came here because of Rosie?'

'No, why would I come here, of all places, because of Rosie? We were worried about Howard. He wasn't at work and Andrew wanted to find him so we tracked him down. His sister lives here.'

Her mum kept looking from the view at the end of the driveway to the house as though the story was making no sense.

A thought occurred to Florence. 'How did you know how to find me, anyway? How did you know where we were?'

'I asked Kimi,' she said. 'You weren't answering your phone this morning and I realised you hadn't got your medication so I took it over and it was obvious you weren't there. Kimi eventually told me you'd gone to Wales and she showed me your text with the picture of the beach. I realised then. I knew why you'd come.' She was crying again. She took her handbag off her shoulder and hunted inside. Her hands were shaking. 'I brought it for you. I thought you must have seen it. You must have remembered.'

'Mum, what are you talking about?'

She pulled a picture out of her handbag. 'The two of you were only three. I didn't think you'd remember but then I thought that maybe it was because it was our first holiday together, the six of us.'

Florence took the photo and studied it, confused. It was a faded colour photograph of her and Rosie playing on a beach. They were tiny. Rosie's hair was still the wild blonde ringlets that'd grown out before she started school. They were wearing similar pink swimming costumes and Florence was holding something out for Rosie to see. There was a castle in the background.

Florence looked up at the coastline below them then back down at the picture again. 'We've been here before?'

'Yes, I thought you knew. We stayed in a cottage near Snowdon and came here for a day trip. It was the only sunny day of the holiday. Wendy and Bob were so annoyed about the rain they insisted we went to Devon every year after that. I recognised it straight away from the picture: the castle and the bay.'

Florence's head was swimming. Her knees were trembling and her legs felt weak. It was the same place.

She stared at the picture. 'I knew it. It felt familiar as soon as we got here.' It was too strange a coincidence and yet it made perfect sense.

Florence and her parents sat on the bench staring at the view. Florence was quiet. She was trying to picture her and Rosie playing on the beach. No matter how hard she tried she couldn't remember. Not that particular holiday on that particular beach. 'It's so weird,' she kept saying.

'To be fair, we visited half of Wales that holiday,' her dad said. 'Remember we went up Snowdon and all we could see were clouds?'

Florence could remember that photograph but she couldn't remember actually doing it.

'Then we spent the day at the place that looks like an Italian village ... '

'Portmerion,' her mum said. 'Rosie dropped her ice cream on the shop floor, remember? Screamed all day long. And where was the castle where we lost her in the gift shop?'

'Harlech. Near that beach with all those tiny conch shells? We could have spent days there collecting them.'

'Shell Island,' her mum said.

'Are they the ones in the pot in the bathroom?'

'Yes, you and Rosie found them. It was near here somewhere.'

Florence was frustrated that she couldn't remember any of it. 'You never told me that we found them.'

'I must have done.'

'We never talk about Rosie any more.'

'No.' Her mum's face fell. 'Maybe we're too worried it'd upset you.'

Florence was staring at the picture in her hands. 'Do you have any more photos from this holiday?'

'Lots. We've got photos from all our holidays. We should get them out.'

'I'd like that.'

Her mum put her arm around her and Florence leant into her, resting her head on her arm. 'I'm sorry we've not talked much lately.'

'Me too.'

'I'll try harder.'

'You're doing just fine. We should be talking to you. I guess I've just been scared to.'

'I'm sorry, Mum.'

'No. We're sorry. We'll all just need to keep trying.'

'Can we have a walk on the beach before we go back?' Florence asked.

'That would be nice.'

'And can Jasper come back with us?'

'Jasper? The one with . . . ' She was floundering for words. She'd been about to say *the eating disorder*.

'With the nice hair?' Florence suggested. 'The big smile? The skinny jeans?'

'Hmm. You want to tell me more about Jasper?'

'Yes, Mum. Yes I do.'

Florence, Jasper, Wilf, Andrew and Megan stood on the beach, taking it in turns to skim stones into the sea. Florence's parents had walked further down the beach. They were holding hands. Florence watched them as though she was seeing them for the first time in a long time.

'They seem nice,' Jasper said.

Florence thought about Jasper's mum and Wilf's dad and felt bad that she hadn't appreciated her own parents more. 'Yeah, they're alright. They just worry so much. It makes me worried too, you know? They're actually surprisingly chilled out today. My mum's even said you should come over for Sunday lunch soon.'

'Sounds good. Did you tell her I'm a cheap date?'

'No, I didn't. I told her you'd charm her. You charm everyone.'

'I don't know about that.'

She snuggled into him and he bent down and kissed the top of her head.

'Put her down, Spider-Boy,' Wilf called out.

'We really should ditch these losers,' Jasper said, smiling down at her.

'I don't think we can now. Andrew has ways of tracking people down.'

'We'll take the motorway home,' Jasper whispered.

When her parents returned they broke apart, laughing.

'It's been a long day and we've got a long trip back to Norwich,' her dad said. 'We ought to be heading off soon. You want me to get you something to eat before we go? Is there anywhere we can get an early dinner, my treat?'

'Hell yes, I'm starved,' Wilf said. 'There's a pub just over the road. We might just need to hide Andrew, I don't think he's in the landlord's good books.'

Florence glanced at her mum. She was looking slightly alarmed and using that *everything's normal, let's not cause a scene* smile. She hoped Wilf wouldn't push her over the edge.

'Yes, Howard said you'd had an interesting time,' she said.

They started walking back to the car park.

'You haven't even heard about Chris Hadfield or the cocaine yet,' Andrew said, his tone matter-of-fact.

Florence looked at Jasper, silently pleading with him to help salvage the conversation.

'Ultimate question, anyone?' Jasper said, then clapped his hands together and pointed a Wilf. 'Favourite pub food?'

'What's an ultimate question?' Florence's mum asked.

'Oh, we just ask each other these silly questions sometimes:

pop culture, favourites and stuff. It kind of breaks the ice at Manor Lane.'

'You mean like who would play you in a film of your life?' Florence's dad said.

'Exactly,' Wilf said. 'Good one.'

'Or what would you call your biography,' Megan said.

'Ooh I like that one,' Florence said.

'Or favourite Doctor Who,' Florence's dad said.

They all said no at once.

'What? Surely that's an ultimate question. It says a lot about a person whether you're a Tom Baker or a Peter Capaldi fan.'

'We've settled that dispute and we're all agreed that David Tennant was the best Doctor Who,' Andrew said.

'Well, I'm afraid I beg to differ.'

'Dad, don't do it,' Florence said.

'In my opinion, Peter Davison was vastly underrated.'

Wilf slapped a hand on his forehead. 'Oh crap.'

Florence, Jasper and Wilf dropped back laughing as Andrew prepared to launch into the biggest lecture of his life.

Florence's notebook

Things That Make Me Joyful

Jasper, my friends, walks down the river, Sunday roasts (especially when Jasper's invited), Wilf's chocolate brownies, Andrew helping me with my homework, the word joyful, looking forward to stuff, hanging out with Kimi, Watson's paws, Converse, my new bracelet from Jasper, planning for uni (even though it's scary), Margot Green's new book, the smell of cut grass, when I hear my parents laughing in another room, Welsh accents (especially the way Megan says the word 'fab-oo-luss'), watching Sherlock, writing poetry (even though mine sucks), new pens with really thin nibs, when people I don't know smile at me in corridors (rare), old movies that go on for ages like Doctor Zhivago, the Desert Island Discs theme tune playing in my dad's study, the colour green, tiny little shells, the sound of rain on a tent, sunlight through trees, otter memes, the smell of Jasper's T-shirt, really fluffy socks, real fires, Christmas lights, brand new notebooks ...

Author's note

When I was a teenager I spent a lot of time reading Judy Blume books. They were the first books I really recognised myself in. The characters were flawed and had worries and home lives I could relate to. They made me feel normal and were a huge source of comfort when the world outside didn't feel very friendly. These were the books that made me want to be a writer. I could never hope to emulate the wonderfully talented Judy Blume but if I could write a book that made just one person feel better about themselves I'd consider that a huge achievement.

The story for *The Definition of Us* was born out of a combination of several different experiences. I guess I am very like my character Jasper: hugely optimistic but occasionally running on excess adrenaline. In my teens I had a couple of experiences which triggered panic attacks and I started to avoid situations that other people found easy. I got to the point where I struggled to go to school and had to speak to the school counsellor. She told me two things that helped me change my perspective. Firstly, when I told her I was worried I wasn't 'normal' she explained that this was not the case. My anxiety was simply a 'normal reaction to an abnormal situation'. For me this was so true. Anxiety is not a personality trait. You're not born with it. It's a natural response that can be explained, treated and overcome. That doesn't mean it's easy, but it *is* possible. She walked me down to a busy, noisy classroom where I should have been having a lesson. I stood outside too scared to go in and she asked me what I was scared of. I told her I was worried I'd have a panic attack in front of everyone. She said with a confident shrug, 'So what if you do?' It was such a surprising statement, so bold and blasé, that it made me laugh and gave me a sudden burst of courage. I walked through the door with that mantra replaying in my head and I still use it sometimes now. I learnt a lot that day but the greatest lesson was that words are powerful, and the right words can change everything.

When I was in my twenties I had three novels published then took a break from regular writing while my children grew up. My son was in and out of school during this time. He was a classic square peg in a round hole. He didn't want to be there. He'd get wound up and frustrated and frequently ran away. When he was nine years old we spent twelve weeks at The Croft, a diagnostic and therapy centre for young people. Most of these young people were out of school and had challenging behaviours. All of them had difficulty making friends, were unhappy and isolated. All of them were interesting, likeable and had many qualities which made them a pleasure to get to know. It made me realise how a mental health, neurological or physical condition can so easily present itself first and mask a person's true personality. What I learnt from this was that a diagnosis does not define a person. No one thing can.

Watching my children grow up and become teenagers has been fascinating. They're questioning, politicised, ideological, complex, hungry all the time, frequently tired and far too stressed. They're also funny. So funny. They're my favourite people to talk to. This book is a conversation with them, with the part of me that has never stopped feeling like a teenager, and anyone who has ever worried whether they're 'normal'. To that I say *So what* if you're not? It's the little things that make you so wonderfully unique that really matter. Normal is overrated anyway.

Sarah x

Acknowledgements

This book would not be possible without the support of many people, both in the publishing world and my personal life. Here are just a few ...

My agent, Yasmin Standen. Editor, Eleanor Russell. Publicist, Sophia Walker. The team at Little, Brown, Piatkus and Atom. David, Ellie and Sam, Mary, Dad, Simon, Mum, Mel, Stephanie, Zia and the staff and families at The Croft Child and Family Unit, Cambridge.

A huge thank you to you all.

Getting help

UK

Advice and support for all kinds of problems

CHILDLINE

Advises, comforts and protects children 24 hours a day
and offers free confidential counselling.

 0800 1111 (24 hours)

 https://www.childline.org.uk/

THE MIX

Information, listening and support for people under 25.

 0808 808 4994 (24 hours)

 http://www.themix.org.uk/

YOUTH ACCESS

Get connected with the right support services and organisations in your area. For anyone aged 11–25.

💻 http://www.youthaccess.org.uk/

SAMARITANS

24 hour confidential listening and support for anyone who needs it (adults included).

📞 116 123 (24 hours)

💻 https://www.samaritans.org/

Information about mental health

YOUNGMINDS

Lots of advice about mental health and how to get help.

💻 https://youngminds.org.uk/

MIND

The mental health charity.

📞 0300 123 3393 (confidential helpline)

💻 https://www.mind.org.uk/

HEADMEDS

Straight talk on mental health medication for young people. Read about others' experiences and get answers to those 'awkward' questions.

💻 https://www.headmeds.org.uk/

B-EAT

The UK's eating disorder charity. They have online support groups and a helpline for anyone under 18.

📱 0345 634 7650 (4pm – 10pm 365 days a year)

🖥 https://www.beateatingdisorders.org.uk/

PAPYRUS

Prevention of Young Suicide, help and advice whether you're worried about yourself or someone else.

📱 0800 068 41 41 (HOPELineUK is a specialist phone service staffed by trained professionals who give non-judgemental support, practical advice and information)

🖥 https://www.papyrus-uk.org

CALM (Campaign Against Living Miserably)

A charity dedicated to preventing male suicide.

📱 0800 58 58 58 (5pm–midnight, 365 days a year)

🖥 https://www.thecalmzone.net/

Drugs and alcohol

FRANK

Confidental information and advice about drugs and
substance abuse, whether it's for you or someone else.

📱 0800 7766 00 (24 hours and it won't show up on your
phone bill)

💻 http://www.talktofrank.com/

Survivors

SURVIVORS OF BEREAVEMENT BY SUICIDE

Confidential helpline for young people over the age
of eighteen.

📱 0300 111 5065 (9am-9pm Monday to Friday)

💻 https://uksobs.org/

SOS SILENCE OF SUICIDE

A place for open, honest discourse by all those affected by
suicide – a safe platform where stigma, shame and silence
do not exist.

💻 https://www.sossilenceofsuicide.org/

SOS: A Handbook for Survivors of Suicide
by Jeffrey Jackson, published by American Association
of Suicidology (AAS): available online, along with other
helpful resources.

    http://www.suicidology.org/suicide-survivors/
    suicide-loss-survivors

Australia

KIDS HELPLINE
Any time, any reason helpline for young people under the
age of twenty-five.

    1800 55 1800

    https://kidshelpline.com.au/

LIFELINE
Provide 24/7 crisis support and suicide prevention services.

    13 11 14

    https://www.lifeline.org.au/

SAMARITANS
A confidential, 24-hour helpline for when life gets too big.

    135 247

    http://thesamaritans.org.au/

SUICIDE CALL BACK SERVICE
Free counselling for suicide prevention and mental health via telephone, online & video for anyone affected by suicidal thoughts, 24/7.

📱   1300 659 467

💻   https://www.suicidecallbackservice.org.au/

SANE Australia
A national mental health charity.

📱   1800 18 7263

💻   https://www.sane.org/

New Zealand

MENTAL HEALTH FOUNDATION
A brilliant collation of the various helplines available in New Zealand that offer support, information and help – including depression-specific helplines, sexuality or gender identity helplines and helplines for young people.

💻   https://www.mentalhealth.org.nz/get-help/in-crisis/
     helplines/

DEPRESSION HELPLINE

A helpline for those struggling with, or worrying about, depression and anxiety.

☎ 0800 111 757

🖥 https://depression.org.nz/

THE LOWDOWN

A helpline for teenagers, covering a variety of concerns.

☎ 0800 111 757

🖥 https://thelowdown.co.nz/

YOUTHLINE

Information, counselling and face to face support.

☎ 0800 376 633

🖥 https://www.youthline.co.nz/

0800 WHAT'S UP

A safe place for you to talk about anything at all – a free counselling service for young people.

☎ 0800 942 8787

🖥 http://www.whatsup.co.nz/